7/23

HARU

ZOMBIE DOG HERO

ALSO BY **ELLEN OH**

Finding Junie Kim
You Are Here: Connecting Flights
The Dragon Egg Princess
Spirit Hunters
Spirit Hunters: The Island of Monsters
Spirit Hunters: Something Wicked
Prophecy
Warrior
King
A Thousand Beginnings and Endings

HARU
ZOMBIE DOG HERO

ELLEN OH

HARPER

An Imprint of HarperCollinsPublishers

To Kiko who, like Haru, would never hurt me even if she turned into a zombie dog. Her brother Tokki, though, would sell me out for McDonald's french fries.

HARU

ZOMBIE DOG HERO

He remembered the first time he set eyes on his human. He'd been a puppy himself venturing from the warmth of his mother's belly when he'd felt a hand grab him by the scruff and place him into a warm and sticky embrace. He looked up into the smiling face of a young boy and felt an instant connection. A sense of belonging.

He licked the boy's face and it tasted sweet and salty, a taste that would forever remind him of this first moment.

"Haru," the boy said. "I'm going to name him Haru because it means 'today.' And I'll call him Haru Haru because he will be with me every day."

It was the first human word he learned.

Haru. His name.

The second was Luke. His favorite word, which meant both his human and his entire world.

CHAPTER 1

Painted Lake, Virginia

THE HEAT OF the blazing summer sun was lessened under
the cooling shade of the copious tree canopy above the trio
of boys marching into the woods. A large black-and-brown
dog bounded ahead, barking in excitement, sending several
chittering squirrels scurrying up tree trunks.

"Haru Haru, come back!" his human Luke shouted from
behind the two other boys.

Haru raced back to rub his body against Luke's before
running around him again.

"Look! It's still standing!" a blond-haired boy named
Max crowed with delight, pointing at the fort they'd made
the previous day. The tentlike structure was backed against

1

the base of a large oak tree with several rafters supporting the main ridge.

"I'll start securing the frame," Max said. Dropping his bag, he pulled out a ball of twine and began to cut it into long strands.

His older brother, Ben, set a big blue bundle next to the fort and began to help Max tie the rafters to the main ridge on the top of the fort.

"Awesome! We can finish it today," said Ben. "Luke, we'll need more sticks before we cover it with the tarp."

Luke nodded and whistled loudly.

"Haru Haru! Fetch big stick!" Luke shouted.

The dog raced off ahead and began nosing the mossy side of a large tree before grabbing a long, thick stick and dragging it over to his human. Luke ruffled his dog's head and sent him back for more. He used a penknife to carve a notch at the end of the stick, which he then passed to Ben. Haru brought back many more sticks that Luke notched while Max and Ben tied them to the main ridge at the top of the fort. When the boys were satisfied with the sturdiness of their structure, they covered the entire frame with the blue tarp Ben had brought and cut off the excess with Luke's penknife.

"Sweet!" Max exclaimed as he high-fived Ben and Luke. "We could camp out here in a rainstorm and be fine."

"No, we couldn't," Ben replied. "The ground would be soaking wet."

Luke grabbed the excess tarp and pushed it inside the fort. "Here, lift up the sides and I'll slide it through."

"Brilliant!" Max enthused. The brothers carefully lifted one side and then the other as Luke slid most of the remaining tarp underneath. Haru sat on the grass and yawned.

"Now we can stay through a thunderstorm!" Max crowed.

"Well, you two can," Luke said with a smirk. "I'd rather be at home in bad weather."

Max shoved Luke on the shoulder. "Wuss."

"Nah, just smart," Luke retorted.

"What's the matter, scared of a little water?" Ben teased. The brothers fist-bumped each other as they laughed.

"Sheesh, I guess you guys aren't hungry and don't want any of these awesome sandwiches and snacks I brought," Luke replied with a smirk, opening up his backpack and peering into it. "All for us, right, Haru?"

Haru cocked his head and barked in agreement.

Max shoved his brother away and immediately slung an arm around Luke's shoulders. "Whatcha bring, best friend?"

Ben blew a raspberry. "Mom said Max would trade us all away for a ham sandwich if he was hungry."

"That's not true," Max responded. "I don't even like ham. But bacon . . ."

On the last piece of tarp, Luke pulled out wrapped sandwiches, chips, cookies, candy, and juice pouches. The boys all sat around the food, Haru pressed tight against Luke's side.

"Turkey and bacon for Max, roast beef and provolone for Ben, ham and cheese for me, and boiled chicken and mozzarella for Haru," Luke said as he divvied up the food. Haru rested his head on Luke's knee.

"Yes! Your parents make the best sandwiches in town," Max said as he took an enormous bite. "Oh man, so much better than the PB&J sandwiches my mom packed for us yesterday."

"I like your mom's sandwiches," Luke replied. "She uses awesome bread and fancy jam and cuts off all the crusts. They're great."

"Yeah, if you're five!" Max complained. "But I'm a man now! I need man food!"

"You're eleven, Max."

"Almost twelve!"

Ben rolled his eyes. "Thanks for all the food, Luke," Ben said. "And thank your parents for us too."

Luke smiled as he watched his friends. He'd met Max in kindergarten, but he'd been friends with both brothers ever since their first time playing together. The Cole brothers looked a lot alike, but they were very different. Redheaded Ben was quiet and reserved, while Max was loud, obnoxious, and could never sit still. Since Luke fell somewhere in the middle of their personality types, they all got along really well.

As usual, Max had wolfed down his food while Ben waited politely for Luke to start eating. This was why his parents preferred Ben over Max. Whenever they came to the store, it was always Ben who politely thanked them while Max raced around, touching everything. Maybe it came with being an older brother.

Max had finished his sandwich and chips and was now looking over to where Haru was delicately eating his sandwich from Luke's hand.

"Haru's looks pretty good also," Max remarked. "Let me have a bite." He reached over as if to take the dog's sandwich, causing Haru to make a cute whiny growl. Turning his back on Max and effectively blocking him, Haru continued to eat his food.

The boys all laughed. It was funny how such a big dog like Haru was so gentle, nibbling carefully around Luke's fingers.

"You can have a Haru sandwich next time," Luke said. "Plain boiled chicken and mozzarella on white bread. I'm sure you'll love it!"

Max made a face, reached for a juice pouch, and squished it. "Hey, it's still ice cold," he said in surprise. "Yesterday our drinks were all warm by the time we drank 'em."

"Well, I froze a whole lot and lined the bottom of my bag with them." Luke turned his backpack upside down on the tarp and a pile of juice pouches tumbled out. "Figured we'd get real thirsty."

Max pressed his drink to his face. "Nice. You must be a genius!"

Grinning, Luke took out a water bottle from the side of his bag and poured ice-cold water in a bowl for Haru before unwrapping his own sandwich.

"I can't believe it's already August," Luke said around a mouthful of food. "School starts in a few weeks."

"ARGH! I'm not listening!" Max slapped his hands over his ears.

Ben shrugged. "I'm looking forward to being an eighth grader," he replied.

Max gave his brother a dirty look. "Only you would say something like that," he groused.

"Don't worry, at least seventh grade is better than sixth," Ben said.

"School sucks no matter what grade it is," Max retorted. "Right, Luke?"

Luke nodded, but truthfully, he didn't mind going to school. He enjoyed his science classes and liked most of his teachers. The only part of school he didn't enjoy was not seeing Haru all day. If Luke had his way, he would take Haru with him everywhere.

Max was now tearing through his second bag of cookies.

"Hey, save some for us, ya greedy pig!" Ben fumed.

"You snooze, you lose—gah! Give that back!" Max lunged at his brother, who'd snatched up all the cookies.

Luke shook his head as the brothers began wrestling over the bags of sweets. There was going to be nothing but crumbs left at this rate.

Suddenly, Haru rose to his feet and began to growl.

"What's the matter?" Luke asked, stroking Haru's tense neck. The growling intensified as the dog continued to stare past the wrestling brothers and into the trees behind the fort.

There was nothing there and yet Haru stood frozen in place, snarling with his hackles raised. Luke was alarmed. What danger was Haru worried about? Luke didn't see anything. He also couldn't hear over the racket his friends were making. Luke stood up and peered around the fort, looking for anything suspicious. Just then he heard an odd high-pitched screeching sound. From behind the fort, a large raccoon staggered into view, chittering and hissing. The animal was disoriented and walking in circles, drooling copiously.

"What the heck is that weird noise?" Max asked as he gave his brother one final shove. He stood up and turned around.

The movement caused the raccoon to bare its teeth aggressively. It charged at Max, causing him to scream and fall to the ground. He kicked his feet wildly, but before the animal could reach him, Haru leapt in front of the boy and grabbed the raccoon by the throat. He shook it like a rag doll before hurling the creature several feet away. Shrieking in rage, the raccoon flung itself at Haru, its lips curled back from its sharp teeth. Haru was barking furiously but let out a sharp yelp at the animal's attack. The raccoon had bitten Haru on the chest and refused to let go.

"Get away from him!" Luke shouted. He grabbed a juice pouch and hurled it at the raccoon, hitting it on the head, but it still hung on to Haru. Luke seized a long stick off their tent and smashed the raccoon on its head, knocking it down to the ground. Dazed, it lay there for a moment. The other boys leapt into action and pelted the animal with anything they could get their hands on. Enraged, the animal turned toward the boys, but this time Haru seized it and flung it hard against the trunk of a tree. The raccoon collapsed, its back legs twitching for a long moment before it went still.

"Haru, are you okay?" Luke knelt at his dog's side and saw blood flowing from a small wound on his chest. "He's bleeding!"

"Don't touch it," Ben warned. "That raccoon probably has rabies. We gotta get Haru to the vet now."

"He saved me," Max said, his voice shaking. He patted Haru's head gently.

"He saved all of us," Ben replied.

Luke was trying not to cry as he clipped the leash on Haru's collar.

"Let's go, Haru," he said.

The hero dog whined as he walked, limping slightly. The boys surrounded Haru as they encouraged and helped him out of the woods. Curious green eyes gleamed from the shadows of the nearby brush. A little white cat watched as the humans left behind the ruins of a battle and the unmoving body of their enemy.

CHAPTER 2

THE SMALL TOWN of Painted Lake, Virginia, was in Manakee County and 195 miles southwest of Washington, DC. It had a population of 8,500 people per the last census and was situated just west of US Route 1, a major highway that traveled up and down the East Coast. Main Street, the biggest thoroughfare, started northeast of town from Route 1 and wound through the picturesque town center until it sharply veered west, past Lake Manakee.

Painted Lake Animal Hospital was south of town, right off Main Street near the lake. Inside, Haru sat in a large cage howling softly to himself.

"Aroo, aroo!" The mournful crooning conveyed the depth of his sadness.

Haru didn't understand why he was here in his least favorite place in the whole world. The VETS. A place where he always got poked with sharp painful things they called the SHOTS. Today's was particularly brutal. It had hurt more than the bite from that sick raccoon.

Haru was sad and confused. He thought he'd done a good thing. He'd smelled the sickness in the creature and knew it was bad for his humans. It was his job to protect them. His human Luke and a whole lot of adult humans had showered him with praise and affection because he'd saved the loud boy from danger. Haru had been happy because he was a Good Boy. The highest of praises. Haru always wanted to be a Good Boy. But then his human parents had left Haru at the VETS instead of taking him home. He hated being in a cage. It was the worst feeling in the whole world. Being trapped and kept away from your family. The VETS were nice to him except when they gave him the SHOTS. It had hurt a lot, even after they soothed him and called him a Good Boy and gave him treats that were yummy. Haru was very unhappy.

The only other time he'd had to stay at the VETS was when he'd been a young pup. He had gotten really sick after eating some human food that had been left outside the back of the store. He remembered seeing the mean woman that always came and harassed his human parents. He didn't like her, but the food had smelled delicious. But he'd thrown up all he'd eaten and yet he had still kept retching, as if everything inside of his body was trying to get out. His humans had been so upset. Luke had cried a lot. Haru had felt guilty. He should have known not to eat the strange food with the small pellets that looked like the color of a bright sunny sky. Such an odd color in his usually gray food. But Haru had recognized the scent of his favorite, chicken, and he couldn't resist. His humans had kept repeating the word "poison" over and over again, so Haru now knew that "poison" was very bad. And now whenever the mean woman came to the store, Haru always growled at her, because she had tried to hurt him.

At least today Haru didn't feel that sick. The pain of his wound had subsided to a dull ache. He would have been perfectly fine at home.

"Aroo, arooooooooo," he whined.

"Calm down, dog, you're bothering me," a large gray cat said.

Haru nosed up against the bars of his cage and stared at the cat, who sat on the long table in the middle of the room, his tail swishing lazily from side to side.

"Why aren't you in a cage?" Haru asked.

"Because I am the boss here," he replied.

Haru was confused. "You are the boss? What is that?"

"The boss. Like my human, who commands this entire

domain. All the other humans must listen to us and do what we want."

"I don't think that's how it works," a calico cat in a small cage on the other side of the room remarked.

"Nobody asked you," the gray cat retorted. He stretched luxuriously and stared at Haru. "Heard you got bit by the rabies."

"What's that?" Haru asked.

The gray cat blinked. "Dog, don't you know anything? The rabies is the dangerous thing that can kill us. It's why we get the SHOTS. Why do you think you're in that cage instead of at home?"

"My name is Haru, not Dog," Haru growled. He suddenly remembered hearing about the rabies being bad. That was why he had to get the SHOTS for it three times. They'd hurt a lot.

"Do I have the rabies now too?" he asked anxiously.

"They don't know," the gray cat replied. "That's why you have to stay in the cage for a little while. Sheesh, don't you listen when the humans are talking about you?"

Haru hung his head. Truth was, he didn't always understand what they were saying.

"If you got the rabies, you may never go home," the gray cat continued.

Haru whimpered loudly. That was the worst thing in the world that could happen. He had to go home to his human.

"Don't pay any attention to what that big hairball has to say. He doesn't know what he's talking about," the calico cat drawled.

"I do too!" the gray cat hissed angrily.

"You're just trying to scare him."

"He should be scared! It's his fault for not being careful!"

A sudden loud growl filled the room. "Be quiet, I'm trying to sleep here!"

Haru peered through the bars of his cage to see a large dark figure not too far away from him.

"Sorry to disturb you," the calico cat said politely. But the figure didn't respond.

"Oh, don't worry about Bruno," the gray cat said. "His family has been going on vacation without him often these days. That's why he's always in a bad mood when he gets dropped off here."

"But isn't vacation a good thing?" Haru asked. Whenever Luke said "vacation," it meant he didn't have to go to school and could stay and play with Haru all day.

"Not when the vacation is at a place that only humans can go," the calico cat chimed in. "My human had to go away for WORK. That's why she left me here."

"Hmph, my human takes me everywhere," the gray cat bragged. "I've even been on the bird machines that go in the sky. Although I really hated it."

"Nobody cares," the calico cat said.

"You're just jealous," the gray cat replied.

A noise at the door caught all their attention as a pretty human girl entered the room. She pushed a cart with bowls of food and a pitcher of water through the open doorway.

"Mitten! Time for din-din!" she caroled.

"Mitten?" The calico cat yowled with laughter.

The gray cat narrowed his eyes.

"You don't get to make fun of my name!" he spat. "What kind of name is Gigi?"

The calico cat stopped laughing and sniffed. "A better name than Mitten."

"I think Gigi is pretty," Haru replied.

"No one asked you!" Mitten snapped angrily before turning away and stalking over to the girl. He began purring as she stroked him.

Haru was suddenly hungry and let out a plaintive woof.

"Oh, I'm sorry, Haru," the girl said, leaving Mitten to plop ungracefully onto his back. "You must be hungry after all you've gone through."

She opened the cage door to give him his food and then sat down to pet him. "You're such a brave dog, Haru. A real hero!"

Not really paying attention to what the human was saying, Haru wolfed down his dinner. The VETS food wasn't as tasty as the food his human mom would make him, but he was too hungry to care. When he was done, he noticed that the girl had left and that the others were quickly eating their food, except for Mitten. Mitten had taken one bite and then turned away.

"What's the matter with your food?" Haru asked. He was still hungry and stared wistfully at Mitten's bowl.

"It's not my normal brand," he sniffed. "I prefer salmon to chicken."

Haru didn't know what salmon was, but he knew chicken was his favorite. His mouth watered, wishing he could eat more.

"Seriously?" Gigi asked. "You are way too spoiled."

The gray cat hissed spitefully at the calico cat.

"Mitten should be grateful that his humans give him any food at all," Bruno growled suddenly. He'd risen quietly and was now glaring at the cat.

The two cats quieted down. Gigi gazed at Bruno in pity. "Are your humans forgetting to feed you?"

"Not forgetting. They're punishing me," Bruno responded. "All because I've been having more accidents lately."

"Oh boy, they really hate that," Gigi remarked. "It's the only time my human ever gets cross with me."

Bruno heaved a mournful sigh. "It's not like I do it on purpose. I'm just getting old, and I can't always control myself. Especially when they forget to let me out. I can't hold it in as long as I used to."

"That's why it's so much better to be a cat," Mitten

responded. "I don't know how you dogs do it. We cats do our business indoors just like our humans. That's the difference between cats and dogs. Dogs serve humans, and humans serve cats because they love us more."

"Cut it out! You're not helping at all!" the calico cat snapped.

But it was too late. Bruno slunk to the back of his cage and curled up into a tight ball.

Haru didn't understand what was going on. He loved being a dog and would never want to be a cat. He had tried to make friends with a little white stray cat that had come into the store once meowing for food. His human mom had sneezed nonstop and got really itchy all over her body, and his human dad had to shoo it out of the store. No, Haru was glad he wasn't a cat. Although he had seen his human dad secretly feeding the cat in the backyard. Afterward, whenever the cat came by, his human dad or Luke would feed it. But if Haru tried to talk to her, she wouldn't say much. The cat was more interested in eating and vanishing into the woods. She wasn't very friendly. Haru attributed it to living in the wild.

"Why do Bruno's humans punish him?" Haru asked quietly.

Mitten stalked over to his cage and began grooming himself. He then stopped and said, "I heard his family received a human baby and spend all their time with it now." Mitten shuddered. "Detestable things, human babies. Always causing problems."

"I quite like them," Gigi said. "They are cute and taste of milk."

"You wouldn't like them if they came into your family and took your place," Mitten warned. "I've heard so many stories like this. The human family brings home a baby and they spend all their time with the baby and forget about their pet. And the next thing you know, their dog is sent to a shelter. Believe me, I've seen it happen often."

The big dog began to whimper.

Gigi snarled at Mitten. "You have a habit of saying the worst possible things!"

Mitten blinked and then continued to groom himself. "Better that he is prepared for the worst."

Haru laid his head on his paws, thinking about Mitten's words. The stray cat that had come to his store had an old collar on, just like Mitten and Gigi and even Haru. The only animals that wore the collars were ones that lived with humans. Was the stray cat abandoned by its humans also? Could his family ever do that to him?

No, they'd never! Haru shook his head hard. Luke was his human and would never abandon him. He was Haru's whole world. He couldn't imagine life without Luke.

Haru spent a restless night and woke up when the pretty human girl came back to let them out of their cages. They followed her out into the large, gated yard with lots of grass and a few trees. After relieving himself, Haru wandered around the length of the fence, staring hopefully through the chain links. As he rounded the perimeter, he came across Bruno staring steadily at the gravel road outside their fence.

"How are you feeling today?" Haru asked.

Bruno didn't respond. He didn't even turn his head, continuing to gaze out onto the roadway. In the sunlight, Haru could see that Bruno was a large black dog with sad droopy eyes. Haru waited next to Bruno for several minutes before getting bored and deciding to move on. At that moment, he heard the loud grumbling of an approaching car and the crunch of gravel.

"They're here!" Haru barked happily. He knew the sound of his humans' car. Running to the far end of the gate, he soon saw the large shiny vehicle turn onto the gravel roadway. Beside himself with excitement, Haru ran back and forth as the car parked and Luke came running to the fence.

"Haru! I missed you so much!" Luke grasped the links of the fence and pressed his face against it.

Haru whined and licked at the parts of Luke's face he could reach.

"Let's go in and get him," Luke's dad said as he reached a finger between the chain links to stroke Haru's nose. Then he pushed Luke toward the building.

As Haru ran for the door into the VETS, Bruno finally spoke up.

"Listen, young one, know this—you can't trust humans,"

Bruno said, turning his sad gaze to Haru. "They will always let you down."

Expecting no answer, Bruno turned back and faced the roadway.

Shaking off Bruno's disturbing statement, Haru ran excitedly to the now-open building door and raced in to find Luke and his dad.

CHAPTER 3

LUKE SAT GLUMLY behind the store counter, staring out at the sheets of rain attacking the front window. It was a miserable day and all he wanted to do was lie in bed with Haru and read his graphic novels. Instead, he was helping his mom mind the counter while she was filling sandwich orders. His dad had gone out for more supplies, but Luke didn't see the need. Not a lot of customers were coming out, because of the rain.

Sun's Deli and Grocery was situated on Main Street a mile north of the town center and was the first place of business one saw when entering the town of Painted Lake. It was housed in a large building with a thrift shop next door and a gas station at the end of the street. Luke and his parents lived in the apartment above the store. Luke liked it because it was big and roomy and whenever he was hungry, he could always run into the store for a snack. He also appreciated that he could see his parents whenever he wanted. And he even liked helping at the store. Well, sometimes.

On a normal day, the store would be busy with customers buying sandwiches and groceries. But other than the mechanics from the gas station, the store had been empty today.

Luke couldn't even have Haru for company. Poor Haru was stuck in the back, since dogs weren't allowed in the main store. Luke was just there to answer questions for customers. If they ever came.

The bell over the door jangled as two wet figures stomped into the store. Luke grinned at his friends.

"This weather sucks!" Max fumed as he shook himself off, spraying Luke with water droplets.

"I can't believe you guys walked over," Luke said. "I'm touched."

The Cole brothers lived a mile south of the store, closer to town proper. It was normally an easy fifteen-minute walk, but it had to have been miserable in the torrential downpour.

"Well, it was stay home and eat cold cheese sandwiches or walk over and get whatever your mom's cooking instead," Ben replied. "A hurricane couldn't stop this guy."

Ben pointed at his brother.

Luke stared at his dripping-wet friends and then at the window that was being inundated with waves of rain.

"I think I would've eaten the cheese sandwich," he remarked.

Max had taken off his raincoat and was now sitting at a table by the window. "This rain is nuts," he said. "It was bouncing off the ground so hard my pants are soaked through. Oh man, I hope your mom made some soup today!"

At that exact moment, Luke's mother appeared, carrying a tray full of food.

"Boys, your mom called to let me know you were coming. She said to stay here and eat and she'd come pick you up in a couple of hours when she gets off her conference call," Luke's mom said as she placed bowls of hearty beef stew and hot-out-of-the-oven cornbread on the table. "Luke, come eat with your friends."

Luke heard Haru whine and saw his head peeking through the back-door window.

"Mom, is it okay if Haru comes out to sit with us since no one else is here?"

Luke's mom looked reluctant but smiled when Ben and Max turned pleading eyes to her also.

"All right, but he has to go in the back as soon as a customer comes in," she said.

Luke raced over to let his dog out and hugged Haru before leading him back to the table, where he was eagerly greeted by Ben and Max.

"It's not fair, Luke," Max complained as he stroked Haru's soft fur. "I wish Haru was our dog. But our mom only likes cats."

"My mom's terribly allergic to cats. But you know you can come and see Haru whenever you want. I'm happy to share him with you," Luke replied. Sitting next to his friend, he began to eat his stew as Haru settled down close, gazing wistfully at the cornbread. Noticing Haru's intense stare, Luke broke off a corner of the cornbread and gave it to him. Haru's tail thumped happily.

"Mmmm, so delicious," Ben sighed as he took a huge mouthful of stew. Then suddenly, he yelled at his brother. "Max, that's my cornbread!"

"Didn't see your name on it," Max replied.

Luke laughed as he saw Max stuff the entire square of cornbread into his mouth. "You're worse than Haru! Don't worry, my mom can make more."

When they'd eaten all the food, Luke raided the ice cream freezer for some ice pops. They sat watching the sheets of rain attack the large front window, with Haru drowsing at their feet. Suddenly, the dog jumped up and stood next to the window, staring intensely outside.

"What's the matter, Haru?" Luke peered out the window

but couldn't see anything.

Luke sat back down, but Haru remained as still as a statue.

"I hate when he does that," Max remarked. "It freaks me out."

"It's probably a squirrel or something," Luke said. But with the rabid raccoon incident still fresh in his memory, he kept a close eye on his dog.

"Hey, did you hear the news about Sinclair?" Ben asked. "He's back in town again. Flew in on a helicopter a few days ago and went straight to his factory. And then there was this huge convoy of armored trucks that arrived. But nobody knows what was in them. They're being really secretive about it. Mom has no idea what's going on and nobody is talking."

Patricia Cole was a reporter for the *Virginia Central*, a local paper. She was fixated on reporting stories regarding Sinclair Industries. Not only was it the biggest company in their town, but Thomas Sinclair was the largest employer in the county and single biggest polluter also. Sinclair Industries was a leading biotechnology company that had expanded to build factories in New Jersey, Delaware, and Maryland. The local factory had originally been for assembly and packaging of vials and syringes. However, about five years ago, Sinclair opened up research laboratory facilities there. But nobody knew what they were researching, because Sinclair was very secretive. And none of the lab technicians who worked there were local.

Max rolled his eyes. "Who cares about that old weirdo?"

"Your mom," Luke retorted. This made all of them crack up.

"Good one, Luke." Max laughed.

"Yeah, it was, but Max, it wouldn't hurt you to actually read Mom's articles you know," Ben said.

"I do read them!" Max replied heatedly. "I read the one about how all the chemicals in his factory are polluting Lake Manakee. And that's why you can't fish there anymore."

Manakee was a large lake that lay southwest of town. It was why their town was named Painted Lake. Because it was so beautiful it looked like a painting. Well, it did, until Sinclair's factory was built on the east side of the lake. Luke thought it should be renamed Polluted Stinky Lake.

"I bet you only read that one because of the picture of the two-headed trout," Luke said, shaking his head. "That was pretty gross."

"Are you kidding me? That was epic!" Max looked outraged. "It was literally split right down the middle with two heads and one tail! How cool is that?"

"This isn't a joke," Ben cut in. "There are people who used to depend on fishing for food but now they can't because all the fish are poisoned. And it isn't from the factory, because the pollution has only happened in the last five years, when they opened up their secret laboratories. Mom says it's companies like Sinclair that are destroying our environment."

Max rolled his eyes. "Oh man, here we go again."

Before the brothers could escalate, Luke jumped from his seat and pointed out the window.

"Whoa! Look at that!" he exclaimed. "What the heck is going on?"

They all crowded close to the window and watched as a large parade of wildlife stampeded out of the woods and down the road in front of the parking lot. It was hard to make out the smaller creatures in the pouring rain, but they saw deer, coyotes, and what looked like a bear run past the store.

"Smoke!" Max shouted as he pointed south.

Even through the rain, they could see massive billowing clouds of black smoke rising high above the tree line.

"Ben, isn't that where the factory is?" Luke asked.

Ben didn't answer as he quickly called his mom. "Mom! I think there's a fire over at the Sinclair factory," Ben said. "We can see the smoke from Luke's store."

Ben's mom shouted loud enough for Luke and Max to hear.

"Unbelievable! I knew this was going to happen! That man is evil. I knew he'd cause an environmental disaster! Ben, you and Max stay inside until I come for you and let me speak to Luke's mom!"

"Okay," he replied before running to the back shouting, "Mrs. Sun, my mom wants to talk to you!"

Max looked over at Luke in concern. "Do you think we're safe here?" he asked.

"I don't know," Luke replied. "We're at least five miles away, but I guess it depends if the fire spreads or not."

He pointed to where Haru was still standing riveted by the front window. "Anyway, I'm pretty sure Haru would let us know if we're in danger."

Hearing his name, Haru's tail wagged as he turned his head to Luke before quickly returning his gaze outside.

"Haru knew the animals were running away," Max said slowly. "Why didn't he warn us to leave then?"

"Maybe because we're inside?" Luke questioned.

"You're right," Ben said as he walked up to them. "Our mom was just telling your mom to keep us inside because of the air quality."

"Why's that?" Max asked. "It's just a fire."

"No, it's much worse," Ben explained. "Because the factory has so many hazardous chemicals, the fire is releasing them into the air."

"So that's why the animals ran away!"

Luke's mom reappeared. She turned off most of the lights, locked the front doors, and put the Closed sign up.

"They just put out an advisory," she said. "They're

evacuating everyone within a mile of the factory and told anyone within five miles to stay inside because of dangerous air quality."

"Welp, if we have to be locked inside anywhere, I'm really glad it's at Luke's!" Max said gleefully.

Luke laughed. "That's because you only think with your stomach."

"I can't help it. I'm a growing boy!"

Luke's mom ruffled Max's hair. "Ready for a snack?"

"Yes, please!" Max nodded enthusiastically.

As Luke's mom brought out chicken nuggets and french fries for the boys to nosh on, she peered anxiously at the sky.

"I really hope the rain stops soon," she sighed.

"Why, Mom? Don't we want it to rain harder to help put the fire out?" Luke asked.

She shook her head. "All this rain is forcing more pollutants into the water, the air, and the earth. It's a terrible situation. It would be better if it was allowed to burn off."

"Oh man, that's gonna cause more two-headed trout," Max remarked.

"Or worse," Ben said grimly.

Luke sat next to Haru and hugged him tight.

CHAPTER 4

SEVEN PEOPLE WERE hurt, and one employee died in the fire. The fire department dug trenches to try to contain it, but it burned for four days and was considered an environmental catastrophe. Massive runoff from the rain had polluted the lake. County officials declared it a disaster site and closed off lake access to the public. Sinclair put out a statement apologizing for the fire and promising to clean it up, but the community was angry. The company had still not cleaned up from the last mess, even after the Environmental Protection Agency had sanctioned and fined them ten million dollars and several local families had sued for an additional five million. It was clear that Sinclair would rather pay the fine and the lawsuits than do the work necessary to become EPA compliant. Luke's father, Peter Sun, explained that it was because actually doing what was necessary would cost over one hundred million.

Around town, the air quality was so bad Luke's mother made him wear a mask whenever he went outside. Luke tried to put a makeshift mask made out of a circle scarf on Haru too, but the big dog would simply swipe it off until Luke finally gave up.

"Well, since you won't wear the mask, you can't stay out and explore like you usually do," Luke admonished. "If the air is bad for me, it's bad for you."

Haru adored Luke and would do almost anything for him, but the cloth Luke kept trying to put over his mouth was too strange.

As much as Haru hated being stuck inside all day, he understood that there was a danger outside. He'd felt the panic of the animals as they fled the forest. The unnatural odors that assaulted his nose were painful and slightly sickening. He worried about the stray cat that visited their store often. He hadn't seen her at all since the fire. It was unlike her to be gone so long. Haru could tell that his human family was worried also. He'd seen both Luke and his father walk out and return with unopened tins of cat food.

After a few days had passed, Haru sensed a familiar presence. When Luke took him out, Haru ran to the shed at the edge of the woods. He had caught the faint whiff of something familiar underneath the acrid stench of the fire.

"Haru Haru, come back!" Luke shouted.

Ignoring his human, Haru went to the rear of the shed and found the little stray cat curled up in a tight ball in the tall grass. Her usually white fur was covered with patches of thick black gunk. It even covered her face. Haru could see how labored her breath was.

Barking loudly, Haru ran to Luke and pulled at his shirt before returning to where the cat lay still.

"Oh no," Luke breathed before shouting for his father. "Dad, the little cat is sick!"

Haru watched as his human dad gently picked up the cat and carried her into the back room of the store.

"What is all the black stuff on her?" Luke asked.

"I'm not sure; the hard stuff looks like tar mixed with petroleum," his dad replied.

"How are you going to get the tar off?"

"Cooking oil should soften it," his dad answered.

"Oh, I saw a documentary at school about animals rescued from oil spills. They used Dawn dishwashing liquid," Luke said. "But you've got to clean her face off first, Dad. She can barely breathe."

"Okay, let's do it."

Haru didn't understand what his humans were saying, but he knew that they would help the little cat. He watched as they put the cat into a large basin to clean her up. His human dad gently washed her face with something soapy. Immediately, she began to breathe easier. They then poured a thick liquid over her body and massaged it into her fur.

"Look, she has a collar and a name tag," Luke said. "Maybe her owners have been looking for her."

His father looked doubtful. "She's been out in the wild for a long time. But if we can get the tar off the tag, we'll see about finding her home."

It took a while, but they were finally able to clean off all the black gunk. They gave the cat water and a little milk, and wrapped her in blankets. During the entire time, Luke's mom had stayed in the front of the store, away from the cat, but she would peer in anxiously to see how she was doing.

"Is she going to be all right?" Luke's mom asked.

Luke gave a thumbs-up sign, which Haru knew was a good thing.

The little cat slept most of the day in the storage room. It was a large room with several rows of shelving filled with store items. In the back, there was a cozy nook underneath a large, grated window with a bean bag covered with lots of soft blankets, where Luke would sit and read with Haru sometimes. Here, Luke had made a space for the little cat with a small bed and litter box. Late in the afternoon, she finally woke up and was able to eat a bit of food.

"How do you feel?" Haru asked.

The cat stretched delicately before responding. "Much better, thank you," she said politely.

"We were very worried about you," Haru continued. "What happened?"

"I was over by the lake," she replied. "There's a family there that always feeds me. But they weren't home. So I wandered over by the factory before the fire and saw something peculiar."

"What was it?" Haru asked.

"The humans there were covered up so that no skin or hair was visible," she said. "They were throwing bags into a large pit. There was a human with a long stick that had fire at the end. He pointed it at the pile and that's when everything went terribly wrong. The fire attacked the human and then spread everywhere. Lucky for me, I was under one of their big moving things or I would have been burned alive. I never saw anything like that before."

"I'm sure you never saw such a terrible fire, either."

"That's true. But I wish the whole place had burned down."

"Why's that?"

"Because it is a bad place. I've seen what they do. Animals go in, but they never come back out."

"What do you mean?" Haru asked.

The cat paused for a long time before finally speaking. "The bags, I could smell what was in them. I know what death smells like."

Horrified at the cat's words, Haru jumped to his feet and paced back and forth for several minutes. "That is a very bad place," he said finally. "You must never go back there."

The cat shuddered. "Don't worry, I won't."

"How did you get covered with that bad stuff?"

"The fire spread so fast, it surrounded me," the cat said. "I tried to escape and fell into a pit full of the sticky substance. I was able to climb out, but not before it got all over me. I am grateful to your humans for saving me. I am aware of how close to death I was myself."

"How were you able to travel so far in your condition?" Haru asked.

"Sheer instinct," the cat responded. "I just knew I had to get as far as I could from the fire. I ran as fast as I was able."

"You were lucky," Haru replied. But Haru was troubled by what the cat had said.

"The animals that went into the bad place," Haru said. "Do you know what kind they were?"

The cat looked at Haru with a pitying expression. "They were mostly dogs."

Haru was shocked.

"But why dogs?"

The cat blinked her big green eyes at him. "How should I know?"

Haru heaved a deep breath. Why was the bad place taking dogs? What had happened to them? And who were these poor dogs? Were they dogs that lived on the streets or dogs like Bruno whose owners might not want them anymore?

The thought sent a chill through Haru's bones. Not for himself, but for Bruno and even the little cat in front of him. The ones who didn't have human families who loved them and would do anything for them. For Haru knew without any doubt that Luke loved him as much as he loved Luke.

He looked down at the cat and wondered what her story was. What had happened to her.

"What's your name?" Haru asked.

"The name my humans gave me before they abandoned me?" the cat asked. "It's been so long since anyone called me it, I'd almost forgotten."

She was quiet for a long time before she said, "Penelope. Penny for short."

"I'm sorry about your humans," Haru said gruffly.

Penelope stretched and blinked. "It was my fault. I scratched their little one when it pulled my tail. And then they threw me away. I was still just a kitten myself and didn't know better."

Haru growled. "That is not your fault. A scratch is no reason to abandon you."

"It was a bad scratch; I caught the child's eye," Penelope admitted.

"Still," Haru said. "It was wrong of them to abandon you."

"That is true." Penelope yawned as she closed her eyes. "You are very lucky to have a good family."

Haru watched Penelope fall asleep before he returned upstairs where Luke was waiting for him. As he snuggled close to his sleeping human's warmth, he thought once again about the cat's sad story and hoped his humans could make a place in their hearts for her.

In the morning, Luke cleaned off the name tag and showed it to his parents as they prepared to open the store.

"Well, it looks like her name might be Pen-something, but the rest of the information is all worn off," his father said.

"Penny?" Luke asked.

His father nodded. "I think Penny suits her."

"Poor thing," his mother sighed. "I thought she was just a feral cat, but it looks like she's been abandoned or lost for a long time."

"Mom, I know you're allergic, but would it be okay if she stays in the back room?" Luke asked.

His mom glanced at his dad before nodding. "If she wants to stay, she is always welcome in the back. But remember, she is an outdoor cat and might prefer that."

"I know, but it would be nice to give her a safe place to stay," Luke replied.

"Well then, when she's here that means you and your dad have stockroom duty!"

"Okay! Come on, Haru, let's go check on Penny!" Luke and Haru ran to the back of the store and into the stockroom where the cat was sleeping.

"Haru, you stay here while I get her food and water," Luke said as he scooped up the empty bowls.

The big dog went to nuzzle the cat, who was now stretching and blinking her eyes awake.

"How are you feeling today?" Haru asked politely.

"I'm doing well," she replied. "But I'm definitely hungry."

"Don't worry, my human Luke is getting you food," Haru replied just as Luke appeared at the doorway.

"Good morning, Penny, you look better today!"

After eating, Penelope drowsed in Luke's lap as he petted her soft white fur and read his favorite webtoons on his cell phone.

"I could get used to this again," she sighed.

"You are welcome to stay here," Haru replied. "I heard the humans talking about it. And I know it would make Luke happy."

The cat snuggled against the boy's stomach and closed her eyes. "It is nice for now, but it never lasts. I've learned that I must take care of myself and not rely on humans."

"You can trust my humans," Haru said.

"No, I can't," Penelope murmured. "I can't trust any of them."

Haru wanted to argue more, but Luke shushed him.

"Quiet, Haru, can't you see she's trying to sleep?"

Upset, Haru dropped into an unhappy heap in front of Luke. He couldn't understand how Penelope could say she didn't trust humans and yet allowed one to hold her so closely. Haru knew that there were bad humans. He'd seen them. He could sense their nature by observing their actions and absorbing their scent, especially evil humans.

But most humans were not bad. Just as he could sense someone's wicked nature, he was keenly aware of when people were good. Even if they were scared of him, he knew. Maybe Penelope had lost the ability to sense good and evil. But then he remembered Bruno from the VETS. He had said something similar. Haru couldn't imagine a life without his family of humans and was suddenly troubled. If he couldn't trust his humans, who could he rely on?

Closing his eyes, Haru fell asleep and dreamed of faceless humans chasing him into a pit.

CHAPTER 5

IT TOOK ANOTHER week and a half for the air to finally clear and be rid of the acrid stench of the chemical fire. The fire department had quickly ruled it an accident and blamed it on the one employee who had died from his burns. The news was met with a lot of anger. Every day, customers would talk to Luke's parents about how disturbing the situation was. No one believed it was just an accident.

"Mom says it really stinks of cover-up," Ben was telling Luke. Ben and Max had come over to hang at Luke's house. They were still not allowed to stay outside, because of the lingering air pollution.

"Geez, everything stinks since the fire," Max cut in. "I wanna know what the heck they were burning, dead bodies?"

Ignoring his brother, Ben kept talking. "That was a

massive fire and it caused a lot of damage and pollution. But Sinclair's just gonna pay some fines and get a slap on the wrist and nothing else will happen to him."

Luke shrugged. "He's rich and powerful and owns almost everything. They're not going to touch him."

"Exactly," Ben replied. "There's gotta be something more to it. Mom says it's way too convenient the way they called it an accident and blamed it all on the Robinson guy who's dead."

"Your mom is investigating it?" Luke asked.

Ben shook his head. "She wants to, but her boss told her to drop it. She's pretty upset."

"Wow, imagine being so rich you could get away with anything," Luke said.

"Like murder!" Max shouted. "I'm telling you, Sinclair's a serial killer and the fire was a cover-up so he could get rid of all the dead bodies."

Ben rolled his eyes, but Luke nodded.

"He may be onto something," Luke said, causing Max to crow with delight. "Calm down, Max, I'm not saying Sinclair's some kind of axe murderer, but what if he did kill someone or do something really awful and used the fire as a cover-up. I mean, I could see that happening."

"Hey, we should investigate it ourselves!" Max said.

"Investigate what?" Ben asked. "We wouldn't even know where to begin."

"I think I know," Luke said.

"You do?" Max asked eagerly. "Where?"

"The factory side of the lake," Luke replied. Pulling out his phone, he showed them a picture of another two-headed fish. "That's where the bad stuff is."

The boys crowded around Luke's phone as they read the article that said the fish had been caught by a local fisherman just the other day, after the county had lifted lake restrictions. It was bigger and more disgusting than the first one. Right underneath the fish's lower jaw protruded another head and gaping mouth. But even more concerning than the two heads was its eyes. The large eyeballs were ringed a bloody red color.

"What kind of zombie-looking fish is that?" Max asked in disgust. "It's gross!"

"The fisherman said both heads kept biting at his hands as if it was possessed. He thinks it would have ripped him up good if he hadn't been wearing gloves," Luke read out loud.

"That's so freaky," Ben said.

"It's the beginning of the zombie apocalypse!" Max intoned in a serious voice.

"Shut up, Max," Ben retorted. "This is important. Why aren't people making a big deal about this?"

"Because old man Sinclair owns everything, including the news stations and your mom's paper," Luke replied. "How many articles has she written that got rejected by her boss?"

Ben nodded. "That's why she's been working on an

exposé. She plans on sending it to the *Times* or the *Post* to get the story national."

"Maybe we can help her by sneaking into the places she can't get into?" Luke asked.

"Let's do it." Max grinned. "I've always wanted to see what's on the other side of the fence."

The factory had a steel wire fence that surrounded the entire property. It was a compound with several buildings.

"You're not seriously thinking of trespassing, are you?" Ben asked.

"Who said anything about trespassing? We're just gonna look around is all," Luke said.

"Yeah, just passing by, like a secret spy," Max sang.

Ben shook his head and sighed. "So, when are we going?"

Later on, when the boys ran downstairs to the store for snacks, Haru went to check up on Penelope and found the little cat itching to return to the outdoors.

"Why do you want to go out? Don't you like it here?"

Penelope licked delicately at her paw before answering. "This is not my home nor my family. And besides, I like living outside. I've gone wild."

"But here you have food and shelter all the time," Haru said. "And you're protected."

"There are delicacies to be had in the wild also, like field mice and little birds, and sometimes if I'm lucky a plump baby rabbit," Penelope said.

Haru drew back, revolted. "That's terrible."

"You only say that because you've never hunted," the cat replied. "There's something powerful and instinctive in hunting prey. It makes the meal so much more delicious."

"That does not sound good to me."

Penelope stared at him unblinking for a long moment. "You are still such a young dog, Haru. You have not seen much of the world. Both good and bad."

"Are you much older than me, Penelope?"

"I am," she replied. "I am well past the midpoint of my life, while you are still growing into your prime."

"Isn't that more reason to stay somewhere safe?"

"I'm not elderly yet!" Penelope said in mock offense.

"But don't you get lonely out there?"

Penelope paused midlick. "Sometimes. And that's when I seek out humans who like to feed me. I get some pets and cuddles and then I'm off again."

Haru shook his head. "That wouldn't be enough for me."

"And that's the difference between cats and dogs," Penelope replied. "We are loners, while you are pack animals."

"I like being part of a pack," Haru responded simply. "I like you. I wish you would stay with us."

Penelope patted Haru gently on his nose. "I like you, too."

From the other room, Haru could hear Luke calling for him.

"Haru Haru, let's go upstairs!"

Haru glanced at the cat, who said, "Don't worry, I'm not leaving yet. I will let you know when I'm ready."

Relieved, Haru rejoined the boys at the back door to go upstairs. Their arms were filled with snacks and drinks, including some liver treats for Haru.

"Were you checking on Penny again, Haru?" Luke asked.

Haru barked in agreement.

"Such a good boy," Luke replied.

Always, Haru thought. He would always be a good boy for his Luke.

CHAPTER 6

SEVERAL DAYS LATER, Luke's parents finally gave the all clear to go outside again, and the boys planned their excursion to the lake.

Lake Manakee was located a few miles southwest of Luke's store, past town, and the factory was on the lake's eastern shore. The plan was for Luke and Haru to walk over to the Cole brothers' house and then they would all hike to the lake.

"Come on, Haru, we're going on an adventure today."

Haru noted that Luke was wearing his big backpack. He could smell the delicious aroma of sandwiches emanating from the bag and he wagged his tail happily. This meant they were going out exploring the world for a long time. Haru loved being outside with Luke just as much as he loved being inside with him.

Luke put on Haru's harness and leash and fifteen min-utes later, they arrived at the Coles' house. Mrs. Cole came out and gave Luke a big hug.

"The boys will be ready in a few minutes. Why don't you come in and wait?" she said.

"No, thank you," Luke replied. "I'll wait outside with Haru."

Mrs. Cole ruffled his hair and went back inside. Luke could hear her shouting for the boys to hurry up.

Max was the first one to come storming out of the house, holding his backpack in front of him.

"What's up, Luke, you got the food?"

When Luke nodded, Max beamed happily. "Cool. I got Mom to buy a bunch of snacks and candy." He opened his backpack to show Luke the hoard of snack-sized chips, donuts, cookies, and candies.

Luke gaped. "Your mom let you take all of that?"

Max looked around, shook his head, and grinned. "But she won't know until after we leave."

Ben appeared and let out an exasperated sigh. "Max, do you ever think of anything besides food?"

"Nope."

Luke chuckled as Ben shoved past his younger brother. Opening his backpack, Ben showed them both the contents.

"I packed a flashlight, rope, my utility knife, binocu-lars," Ben said. "I couldn't think of anything else except a camera, but we all have our cell phones."

"Good job!" Luke replied. "Let's go!"

Ben put a hand on his friend's shoulder. "Are you sure about this?"

Luke nodded. "And if we find something, maybe your mom can write the story up. Bad people shouldn't get away with bad things just because they're rich."

The friends walked the entire length of Main Street all the way through town, stopping after an hour to sit at Red Leaf Park near their old elementary school to eat their lunch. Afterward, they took Main Street to the outskirts of town and then turned down Lake Manakee Drive, a winding scenic road that led to the lake.

When they arrived, Luke was struck with how much had changed in the last few years. He could still remember when they would go to the lake to swim and fish. Families lined up all along the lakeside to enjoy a picnic. Now the lake was completely empty of people. The dock where boats could be rented was abandoned, the empty pedal boats still bobbing in the water. And where there used to be tons of ducks and geese, now there was hardly any wildlife.

"Whoa, we haven't been here in a few years. Since they found that first two-headed trout," Ben commented. "It's got some serious ghost town vibes now."

"This place used to be so much fun," Max said sadly. "Sinclair messed up all the good things."

The three boys turned and looked at the Sinclair compound. It had shut down completely after the fire, and the older buildings, including the factory warehouse and the original laboratory, looked ruined. However, the taller, newer laboratory building seemed less damaged. As they approached the wire fencing that surrounded the compound, they were hit with a horrible stench.

"Blech! What the heck is that smell?" Max gagged.

"Whatever it is, it's coming from the factory," Luke said as he held his nose.

"It smells like death and diarrhea!" Max whined. "Let's get out of here."

Haru began to growl deep in his throat, his eyes fixed on the building.

"See, even Haru is warning us to get away!" Max insisted.

"No, wait," Ben said sharply. "Look! There's something going on!"

The boys rushed to where a line of trees bordered the fence. Luke hushed Haru, who was still growling.

Kneeling in the tall grass, Ben quickly pulled out the binoculars.

"That's really odd," he said. "I thought nobody was supposed to be working right now."

"Yeah, didn't they say it was too dangerous?" Luke asked.

Ben passed the binoculars to Luke while he pulled out his phone and began filming. Luke peered through the binoculars and watched as an unmarked black van pulled up next to the laboratory building. Several men in silver hazmat suits exited the vehicle. Once again Haru started growling.

"Quiet, Haru," Luke whispered. "We don't want to get caught."

Luke watched as the men went down a staircase that led to what seemed to be the basement of the laboratory building. Suddenly, they heard dogs barking and whining before the sound was cut off abruptly, as if a door had opened and closed.

"Did you hear that? What's with all the dogs?" Max asked.

Luke and Ben looked at each other in alarm. Haru stood with his hackles raised, staring intently at the building.

"Do you think they're experimenting on dogs?" Ben asked.

Luke shuddered at the thought. "He can't be that awful, can he?"

"Oh yes, he can," Ben retorted.

"That's animal cruelty! We've gotta report him!"

"Yeah, but for what?" Ben asked. "We don't know what's happening in there, and look at all the security guards. There's no way we're getting inside to find out."

Luke bit his lip. Just the thought of dogs being locked up in the laboratory was upsetting him. "Well, they're supposed to be shut down, but clearly they aren't! Your mom could investigate that, right?"

"Yeah, and all those dogs. It sounded like there was a lot of them! What are they doing to them?" Max asked.

"It's all so shady. The hazmat suits, the awful smell." Luke stopped as they all went quiet. "They're experimenting on the dogs, right?"

Max shuddered. "We've gotta stop 'em!"

"Don't worry, I got it all on video," Ben replied. "Mom will know what to do."

Next to them, Haru began growling. The boys quieted in alarm, but it was too late.

"Hey, you kids! What are you doing over there?" A security guard was heading toward them.

"Quick, let's get out of here!" Luke grabbed Haru's leash and pushed his friends to move. They all bolted for the road, leaving the guard shouting at them through the fence. They didn't stop running until they were back on Main Street heading into town.

Out of breath and hot and tired from their frantic running, the boys collapsed under the shade of some trees by the side of the road to catch their breath and drink some water. Max pulled out a pack of powdered donuts and methodically stuffed them into his mouth.

Luke poured cold water for Haru as they rested.

"Let's call Mom to pick us up," Max whined, white

powder covering his mouth. "I'm too tired."

Ben nodded. "That's not a bad idea," he replied. "We have a lot to tell her."

Luke hugged Haru tight as he thought of the poor dogs trapped in the burnt shell of the building. "I won't ever let that happen to you," he whispered.

CHAPTER 7

THE BOYS EXPLAINED everything they had seen to Mrs. Cole when she picked them up. Luke could see sharp curiosity overtaking the anger in her eyes, even as she scolded them for going to the factory.

"That was a dangerous thing to do," Mrs. Cole said. "They closed off that area for a reason."

She paused and then turned to look at each of them. "But you've raised some very interesting issues. I think I'll drop you off at Luke's place and go back to snoop around."

"The dogs," Luke reminded her. "We have to help them."

She returned an hour later with a grim look on her face.

"I went around the factory and saw people in hazmat suits exiting the laboratory building," she said. "When I went to the entrance, the security guards wouldn't let me in, and I couldn't find anyone willing to talk to me. Nobody from their press office is returning my calls, and when I finally got a higher-up on the phone, they claimed that the factory is currently nonoperational and no one is there but security. But that was clearly a lie."

"What is it, Mom? What do you think is happening?" Ben asked.

"I don't know, but I intend to find out," Mrs. Cole replied.

After the noisy boys and their mother left, Luke had to help in the front of the store and Haru went to spend time with Penelope.

The cat was napping but became completely alert when he arrived. She sniffed him delicately when he went to greet her.

"You smell of the bad place," she said.

"Yes," he replied. "I went with Luke and his friends."

"Why did you go there?" Penelope asked. "It isn't safe for you especially."

Haru thought of what he had seen there and agreed. "You were right. Something terrible is happening there. I heard the dogs. They were in pain and crying for help. But I didn't know what to do."

"We can't help them," Penelope replied. "The important thing is for you to stay away from there, or you will die."

Haru was silent. In his mind, he could still hear the pleas

of the dogs, asking to be released. The pain and fear in their voices. The anger and the sadness. He'd heard it all and he'd felt powerless.

"The humans will save them," Haru said. "Luke will tell his parents and they will save the dogs."

"Haru, you are still young and have not seen much of the human world," Penelope replied with a pitying look. "There is a hierarchy in their society. Your humans, as lovely as they are, do not have power. They will not be able to save those dogs."

"What do you mean, power?" Haru asked.

Penelope stood up and stretched. "Who is the leader of this family?" she asked.

"Mother and Father," Haru responded quickly. "They are both leaders, but sometimes I think Mother is the real leader because when she's not happy, no one is happy."

Penelope smirked. "That *is* power. And yet, I have seen other humans come and yell at them."

Haru growled. "I hate when that happens."

"Because they are your family and you love them," Penelope agreed. "But outside of this building, they are merely humans with no greater power than the others."

"Then what makes some humans powerful? Because they are stronger?"

"Yes and no," the cat replied. "For I have seen a small and gray-haired old human who was so frail, he would fall over if I jumped on him. And yet he wielded power over many who were much younger and stronger than he."

"How is that possible?"

Penelope wiped her face gracefully before answering. "Some humans hold the ability to control others."

This reminded Haru of the conversation with Mitten at the VETS. He had said he was the boss.

Boss. Like my human, who commands this entire domain. All the other humans must listen to us and do what we want.

"So that is what 'boss' means," Haru said.

"Yes, that is a word that they use to mean that a human is above them," Penelope said. "They are strange that way. It isn't strength that is important to them. I've never figured out what it actually is. But it is so odd that a human who would not survive a day in the wild can still be their leader."

"Are these boss humans good people?"

"They are just like animals. Some are good, some are bad. But the more powerful they are, the more evil they seem to be," Penelope explained.

"I don't understand what their power is," Haru bemoaned. "What is more powerful than strength?"

"My understanding is that it is an item that they worship," Penelope said. "All humans want it and need it. Sometimes they will do bad things to get it. And the more they have, the more powerful they are."

"I wish I had some," Haru said.

"Why? It is a useless thing for animals," Penelope said. "It is only humans who worship it."

"Well, I could give it to my humans so they could be powerful too," Haru said. "At least they would be good bosses."

"Yes, they would be better than the evil human I saw," Penelope responded darkly. "He is the boss for the bad place near the lake. I've seen him there many times before. Everyone was running to do his bidding. He controls them all."

Haru growled. "Then he is the reason the dogs are there!"

"And that is why your humans won't be able to do anything," Penelope remarked. "He has many more people that do his bidding. They cannot fight him."

Haru slumped down on the ground. "I do not understand the human world."

"We are not supposed to," Penelope sighed. Stepping out of her little bed, Penelope walked over to Haru and cuddled up against his side.

"Don't go over there again," she said. "I don't want to see you get hurt."

Haru licked the top of Penelope's head affectionately. He was going to really miss her when she left.

CHAPTER 8

THE WORST DAY of Haru's life started with Penelope's disappearance early in the morning. He could hear Luke calling for her, but Haru knew she was gone. He sensed it as soon as he woke up. She had left them. It wasn't a surprise, but Haru was filled with sadness.

"Dad, Penny's gone!" Luke shouted.

His father was making the morning coffee and preparing to open up the store.

"Yes, I thought I saw her slip out last night when I was taking out the garbage," his father said.

"But why didn't you stop her? What if she gets hurt again?" Luke was upset.

His father placed a comforting arm around Luke's shoulders. "I know you wanted to keep that little cat safe, but I

58

don't think forcing her to stay is the right thing. I think she's more comfortable in the wild."

Luke looked angry as he called for Haru to follow him outside. They searched the entire back woods for the little cat, but she was gone. Her scent trail was too faint to track.

Seeing how worried Luke was, Haru wished Penelope hadn't run away, but he knew that she'd been set on returning to the wild. He could only hope she would continue to visit as usual.

In the early afternoon, the heat grew sweltering and Luke and Haru stayed in the back of the store because it was the coolest place in the building. With nothing to do and no customers coming into the store, Luke began one of the new graphic novels he'd borrowed from the library, *Superman Smashes the Klan*. Just as he became absorbed in the 1946 setting of the story, he heard Haru start to growl and then the nasally voice of his least favorite person. Opening the door to the store just a crack, Luke could see Mrs. Sinclair-Greene, one of the largest landowners in the entire county and the store's landlady. She was Sinclair's cousin and extremely proud of that relationship. She was also a terribly nasty woman who liked to come by and harass all her tenants for no other reason than boredom. Today, she wore a black dress with some fur shawl, and her dyed blond hair was swept into a tight bun.

"I am here to tell you something important," Mrs. Sinclair-Greene said as she helped herself to a cheese Danish from the glass container on the counter. "But first a black coffee," she said as she took a huge bite of the Danish. She then sat down at the table, expecting to be served.

Whenever she came into the store, she would help herself to drinks and food without asking or paying. She acted as if everything in the store was hers, just because she was the landlady. And Luke's parents could never say anything to her.

After she scarfed down the Danish and drank her coffee, she wiped her hands on a napkin and threw it on the floor. Standing up, she said, "I am increasing your rent with the new lease." She passed a piece of paper to Peter.

Luke's mom gasped and his dad crumpled the paper in anger. "This increase is outrageous! We don't make enough revenue to justify it!"

"I can't help it if you aren't good at your business," Sinclair-Greene replied. "Maybe it's because you're foreigners that you don't have customers."

Luke balled his hands into tight fists that shook with rage as he listened from the back room. He could see how angry his father was and how his mother was trying to calm him down.

"Ma'am, my wife and I were both born and raised in this country. We are Americans, not foreigners."

"Whatever," Sinclair-Greene said with an uncaring wave of her hand. "I should've never agreed to rent to you people in the first place. Maybe I'll just tear up the lease renewal and get one of those coffee franchises in here. It would suit the aesthetic better with the antique store next door."

Luke rolled his eyes. It was a huge stretch calling the thrift store next door an antique shop.

Lydia Sun pushed her husband back as she leaned forward to speak with the landlady.

"Please don't do that, Mrs. Sinclair-Greene," she pleaded. "You know that we just invested a lot of money into renovating the whole store last year."

"That's your problem, not mine," the landlady retorted. "But as long as you pay me the new rent price, you can stay."

"But it's too high," Lydia said. "And it's been a hard time for a lot of local families these days. We've had to extend credit to many of our longtime customers."

"How stupid of you! That is exactly why your business is failing!"

"The whole community is hurting because of the economy!" Peter burst out. "We're not asking you to give us a discount. We're just asking you not to raise our rent right now."

"You foreigners are all the same! Always looking for handouts or trying to cheat decent hardworking Americans," she spat out. "You people should have never been allowed into this country in the first place!"

At her words, Luke could see the terrible hurt and anger on his parents' faces. Unable to control himself, Luke shoved the door wide open and rushed toward the landlady.

"You're a horrible, awful woman!" Luke shouted as he

ran toward her. He stood in front of her, glaring. His hands clenched into tight fists.

"How dare you talk to me this way, you disrespectful boy!" Mrs. Sinclair-Greene fumed.

"Luke!" his father admonished. "Please go to the back, this is not your concern."

Ignoring his father, Luke continued to lash out at Mrs. Sinclair-Greene. "You shouldn't talk to my parents that way! You are a racist, ugly old witch!"

Mrs. Sinclair-Greene narrowed her dark eyes and pursed her lips. "You are a nasty little boy who deserves to be whipped," she said. And then she slapped Luke hard across the face.

Luke reeled back in surprise. No adult had ever hit him before. But before anyone could react, Haru came rushing from the back room, barking furiously. Luke stopped him before he got too close to the woman, but as Haru snapped his teeth at her, she flung herself backward with a scream and fell against the shelves filled with chips and cookies. The whole shelf crashed to the floor, taking her, shrieking at the top of her lungs, along with it.

Luke's parents rushed to help her, but Mrs. Sinclair-Greene slapped their hands away, still screaming hysterically. Her driver ran into the store to help her up.

"Hughes, call the police this instant! Tell them I've been attacked by a vicious dog!"

"Please, ma'am." Luke's father tried to calm her down.

"Get away from me!" she shrieked. Searching through her bag, she found her cell phone and made a call. "Is this animal control? Come immediately to Sun's Deli! I've been attacked!"

"He didn't attack you! You just fell back," Luke tried to explain.

But she refused to listen. Her right arm was scratched and bleeding from the fall, and she kept shouting that the dog had attacked her.

"Did Haru bite her?" Luke's dad asked quietly.

"No, Dad," Luke said. He was crying, his arms tight around Haru's neck. "He lunged at her, but I held him back. He never touched her."

"It's okay, son. I couldn't see, but I believe you. We'll explain that to the officer. You go take Haru to the back and wait for us."

Within thirty minutes a police officer and two men from animal control appeared. Luke recognized Officer Blake from career day at school. He was a tall, handsome Black man who was his friend Lamar's father. But the other two white men in gray uniforms were new to him. Luke listened from the back room as Mrs. Sinclair-Greene lied about Haru, showing her bloody arm as proof.

"That is a dangerous dog! This is not the first time it has acted aggressively toward me. Every time I come here, I am in fear for my life! I want this dog removed from my property!"

"Mrs. Sinclair-Greene, technically this is their store that they are leasing from you. They are allowed to keep their dog here," Officer Blake explained.

"Then I will terminate their lease this instant, for public safety!"

"Please, ma'am, you can't do that!" Lydia cried out in alarm.

"Either the dog goes, or I will not renew your lease and I'll have you evicted immediately!"

As Luke's mom pleaded with the landlady, the police officer pulled Peter aside.

"We got ourselves in a pickle over here," Officer Blake sighed. "She can't technically evict you without a court order. But she may argue that Haru is a dangerous animal on her property as a legitimate reason for why she won't renew your lease."

Luke rushed over to the policeman. "Haru isn't dangerous. He's a good dog! He's a hero! Please don't let her take him away."

Officer Blake patted Luke gently on his shoulder. "I know, son. We all know Haru is a good dog."

"Then please help him!" Luke begged.

Officer Blake sighed and faced Luke's dad again. "Listen, Peter, you know how the Sinclairs can be. Why don't we let animal control take him to the pound for now and we'll clear up this whole mess tomorrow in front of the judge?

It's the only way I can think of to get her out of your hair right now."

Luke's dad nodded reluctantly.

"NO!" Luke screamed. "I won't let you take him!"

Luke ran back and put his arms around Haru. Even as his father tried to pull his arms away, he refused.

Haru was very confused and worried. He didn't mean to make the awful woman fall; he just meant to scare her for hitting Luke. As much as he disliked her and knew that she had tried to poison him when he was young, Haru knew better than to bite any human. He knew he hadn't even touched her. All he'd done was lunge and snap his teeth. But he could tell he was in trouble from the way the mean woman was screaming and carrying on. Now men in strange uniforms had come into the store, and two were coming toward him with some kind of contraption. He tried to hide behind Luke, but his human dad pulled Luke away.

The men suddenly looped a muzzle over Haru's head, causing him to whine and struggle.

"Haru! Haru!" Luke was screaming and crying. Like Haru, he was struggling against his parents, who were holding him back.

Haru was scared. He hated to see Luke crying. He needed to comfort his human, but they were dragging him out of his home. They were taking him away from his family. He couldn't bark but he growled and fought, lashing out with his legs. It was no good; they were too strong for him. They carried him out of the store.

Luke went running after them. Trying to get to Haru.

"Don't hurt him!" Luke screamed as he pulled at the man's arm. The man shoved him away, causing Luke to fall hard on the ground. Haru growled and flailed mightily. But the men locked him in a cage inside the van.

"You know where to take him," the mean woman said to the men.

The men nodded and got in the van.

"You're a horrible person! I hope something terrible happens to you!" Luke screamed.

"Luke!" his father yelled sharply. "Don't say that!"

"What a nasty child!" Mrs. Sinclair-Greene sneered. "You'd like it if I terminated your parents' lease, wouldn't you?"

"He's just a child," Luke's father pleaded.

Luke tore away from his father's arm and ran after the van as it headed down the road. He could hear Haru barking and saw his dog staring back at him through the windows.

"Haru!" Luke shouted, frantically running after the van. "Don't take my dog! Don't take my Haru!"

The van sped out of the parking lot and down the road. Luke chased it all the way out to the road, where he tripped and fell hard on his knees, sobbing. Peter ran over and picked Luke up.

"Dad, you have to take me to the pound right now! I have to be with him. I don't want him to be alone. I don't want him to think we sent him away."

Peter exclaimed over the blood covering Luke's knees, but Luke shook his head. "I don't care about that! I need to go to Haru!"

"Okay, let's close up the store and we'll go right away."

As they returned to the store, they watched as a smirking Mrs. Sinclair-Greene got into her car and drove away.

"I hate her," Luke whispered.

His father put a comforting arm around him as he led him inside, where Officer Blake was finishing up his report.

"I'm so sorry about all this," Officer Blake said. "But I'll let Judge Hopkins know, and do what I can to help you get Haru home again."

"Thank you," Peter said, shaking the officer's hand.

Luke was too devastated to respond. All he could think about was Haru.

CHAPTER 9

THE POUND WAS on the south side of town. It took fifteen minutes for Luke and his father to drive to the location. As soon as they arrived, Luke noticed that the van that had picked up Haru was not there.

"I don't understand. They should have gotten here before us," Peter responded.

Luke hurried inside and listened nervously as his father asked the front desk about Haru.

"I'm sorry, the van hasn't arrived yet," the receptionist said. "But they may have taken him somewhere else because we are completely full."

"Where'd they take him?" Luke asked in a panic.

"Let me find out," she replied.

They waited as she called. "I don't know what is going on. No one is picking up."

Luke turned his panicked eyes to his father. "Dad, where's Haru?"

He could see the anger and determination on his father's face. "It's all right, son. We're going to find him."

Turning back to the reception desk, Peter asked, "Is it all right if we wait here for them to return?"

The woman nodded and waved them to the front seating area, where they sat on uncomfortable plastic chairs. As they waited, Luke texted Ben and Max to tell them what had happened. Too agitated to talk to his friends, Luke ignored their calls. A minute later, Mrs. Cole called Luke's father to ask what had happened.

Luke could only think about how scared and confused Haru must feel. He needed to see Haru and hug him and let him know that he still loved him. He needed to let Haru know that he would do anything and everything to be with him again.

Two hours passed and the van had still not returned.

"I'm sorry," the receptionist said when they approached her again. "It looks like they must have gone home for the night. You'll have to come back tomorrow."

"Can't you ask them where they took Haru?" Luke asked.

She hesitated. "I haven't actually talked to them. They aren't answering their phones."

Luke bit his lip and stared up at his father.

"Is there any way you can tell me where to find them?" Peter asked.

"I'm sorry, sir, but I can't give out personal information."

Outside the pound, Luke crouched down on the ground, fighting back tears.

"Don't worry, son, we'll find him," his father said. "If we have to go to every shelter in the state, we'll find Haru and bring him home."

"You promise?" Luke asked, his voice trembling in anguish.

"I promise I'll do everything in my power to get Haru back," his father said.

Wiping away his tears, Luke clung to his father's hand as they headed home.

There he found Ben, Max, and their mother talking with Lydia.

Ben and Max raced over to Luke's side, their faces reflecting the same anguish Luke was feeling.

"Mom said she'll do anything she can to help," Ben said as he put an arm around Luke's shoulders. "Don't worry, we'll find him. Mom has a plan."

Max nodded and patted Luke's shoulder, but for once he was completely silent.

"I looked it up and there are fifteen animal shelters that the van could have possibly gone to," Mrs. Cole was saying as she passed a list to Luke's father. "We can check back at the local shelter in the morning and if there's still no sign of Haru, we should split up this list and start looking."

"Thank you, Patricia," Peter said. "This is a huge help."

"Don't mention it. Haru saved my boys. I'll never forget that," she replied. Hesitating, she glanced over at Luke before continuing. "Peter, don't you think it's so strange that those two men disappeared with Haru and the shelter is claiming they never came back? That part is really bothering me."

"Yes, it feels nefarious."

"Exactly. Something's definitely up."

Max leaned over to Ben and asked, "What's 'nefarious' mean?"

"Evil," Ben whispered, with an apologetic look at Luke.

"Poor Haru," Max sighed. "I hope he isn't like those dogs that got sent to the factory."

Ben hit Max hard in the side with his elbow, causing Max to let out an "Ooof!" But it was too late. At his words, Luke began to panic.

"Dad! What if they took Haru to the factory? What if they're experimenting on him! Like all those other dogs! We have to go there now! We have to find Haru!"

"Luke, I don't understand what you're talking about." Peter looked perplexed.

"They were there! Hundreds of dogs! And men in hazmat suits, and there was a terrible smell. What if Haru was taken there?"

Mrs. Cole reached over and grabbed Luke's hands. "Honey, you have to calm down. I don't think Haru was sent to the factory. It was animal control that came for him. They would never do something like that. I'm sure he had to have been sent to a shelter. We'll find him tomorrow. Don't worry."

Luke was visibly trembling and fighting back tears. "If anything happens to Haru, I will never forgive myself," he whispered.

Ben and Max surrounded their friend. "Don't worry, Luke. He's going to be fine."

CHAPTER 10

HARU PACED BACK and forth in the cage, sometimes falling down when the van hit a bump in the road. He didn't know where the men were taking him. He wanted to rip the muzzle off his face. He wanted to bark his head off and warn these men that they would be in deep trouble if they didn't take him back to his family. But Haru was helpless. For the first time in his life, he was really scared and didn't know what to do. He just wanted to be with his family.

He could hear the men talking and laughing and he growled at them. One of the men yelled at him to be quiet.

"Stupid dog, you're giving me a headache! I swear, Jim, it's a good thing this is our last job for that nasty hag! I really hate dogs," the yelling man complained.

"Oh, for crying out loud, Stan, how many times I gotta

tell you, we're done picking up the dogs for now, but we still gotta deal with them in the lab, ya nincompoop."

"But I hate dogs," Stan whined. "Can't we find a different job?"

"No, we can't," Jim said sternly. "This is the best-paying job we can get and you'd better not mess it up for us, Stan, or I swear I'll disown you."

"Aw, come on, Jim, you promised Mom on her deathbed that you'd always look out for me," Stan responded.

"What do you think I'm doing, ya big doofus? This here job is the best money we've ever made. We ain't losing it, ya hear?"

It was quiet in the van, except for Haru's soft whines.

"That old lady scares me," Stan said after a minute.

"Well, that's one thing you don't have to worry about," Jim said.

Stan brightened up. "Really?"

"Yeah," Jim replied. "Now we gotta deal with old man Sinclair instead."

Stan sunk down in his seat. "That ain't better! He scares me more!"

"You hush up before I give you something to really be scared of!"

Haru didn't understand anything the two bad men had been saying, but he smelled their destination minutes before they arrived. The horrible unnatural decaying funk of the bad place was immediately recognizable. Filled with dread, Haru growled louder, pacing faster in the cage. He was not supposed to be here.

As they pulled up to the gates of the factory, a security guard with a face mask waved them in.

"P-U! I ain't never gonna get used to that nasty stank!" Stan said, holding his nose. "We really need to get a new job, Jim."

"Just put on the suit!" Jim yelled as he parked the car.

The two men got out of the car and put on the hazmat suits that were in the back next to Haru's cage. Then they lifted the cage onto a cart and pushed it into the building, down a dim hallway to a large freight elevator.

Terrified, Haru whined loudly.

"Shut up!" Stan shouted as he banged on the cage.

Haru shrank back in fear, whimpering. He stayed quiet as they loaded him onto the elevator and pushed a button. When the heavy metal doors reopened, the first thing Haru heard was the clamor of dogs. The din was overwhelming. Haru curled into a tight ball, shaking. The men pushed the cart down the hallway, past doorways that sounded of frightened, imprisoned dogs. Then they stopped at the end of the hall and entered a large room. Haru had never seen a place like this. The room was sectioned off into two areas. One was a large glass-encased room with several people wearing white coats like at the VETS. They wore big glass things on their faces and seemed very busy. The other half of the room was lined with cages containing dogs. In the very back of the room were several empty glass boxes surrounded by big machines that let off a low droning noise. A host of humans were monitoring the machines. One of them, a very tall person in a shiny suit, approached Haru's cage.

"What are you doing here? We don't need another dog right now."

"Look, Dr. Hawley. Mrs. Sinclair-Greene told us to bring this dog straight to you," Jim replied. "She said this one is real strong, perfect for the new strain."

The tall man peered through the bars to stare at Haru. Even without seeing the man's face, Haru could sense the malevolence emanating from this human. Here was a person who was evil and would think nothing of harming him. Haru growled as fiercely as he could.

"All right, put him in number five. We'll use him first."

Haru was pushed to the area where large cages were lined up against the wall. He could see a few dogs barking wildly at their approach.

"Open up that empty cage in the middle, Stan, and be quick about it!"

The bigger human unlocked the cage door and then turned to open Haru's. Seizing him by the muzzle, Stan threw Haru into the new cage and slammed the door.

"You forgot to take the muzzle off, ya dimwit!" Jim yelled.

"I ain't doing it! He'll take my hand off, just watch!" Stan yelled back. "Why can't we just leave it on?"

Jim shoved Stan out of the way. "He needs to be in good shape for the test. Which means he gotta eat and drink, ya big doofus."

Opening the cage, he reached in and unclipped the muzzle. As soon as Haru felt it release from his head, he tried to bolt out the door, but the man whipped out a long orange stick that sent a shock of electricity through Haru's body. Whimpering in pain, Haru crashed into the back of the cage.

The man chuckled. "Now, that's how you keep these dogs in check."

"Shoot, I want one of those cattle prod things too, Jim."

"You'll get one soon enough. But you need to be gentle with it. Too much juice and the dogs won't be no good for the tests and them scientists will be real mad," Jim said.

The human Jim locked Haru's cage, and he and the other, bigger man pushed the cart away and out of the room.

Haru lay shivering in his cold cage. He closed his eyes in pain and wished for his family.

"Hey, new dog. You okay?"

"He's definitely not. You know how much those hot sticks hurt."

"Tell me about it! Makes me want to bite their hand off when they use it."

"Makes me want to hot stick their faces!"

Canine laughter caused Haru to open his eyes in curiosity. To his left was a large Doberman and behind him in another cage was an even larger German shepherd.

"What is this place?" Haru asked.

"Welcome to the Death Dungeon," the Doberman replied.

"Dogs come in, but they don't come out," the German shepherd cackled.

"Not alive, at least." The two dogs keened in laughter that also held a sharp edge of hysteria.

"Leave him alone," a growly voice snapped.

Recognizing the voice, Haru jumped to his feet and turned around. In the cage next to his lay Bruno.

"Bruno! Why are you here?"

Bruno turned his sad brown eyes to him. "I told you, young one. Never trust humans. I hate that I am right. Your family abandoned you too."

"No, they didn't. They tried to keep me, but I caused an accident and those bad men took me away from my family against their will. I know they will come find me and take me home."

At his words, the Doberman and German shepherd howled with laughter.

"No dog leaves the dungeon!"

"Except in a doggy bag!"

Haru stared, mystified by their ghoulish humor.

"Don't mind them," Bruno said. "They're longtime

strays that were here before me. Dark humor is how they keep from losing their minds like that one." He gestured to a dog on his other side. It was an Irish setter that stood staring into space, his entire body visibly trembling, his eyes twitching uncontrollably.

"When did you get here, young one?" Bruno asked.

"Just today," Haru answered shakily. "My human must be very upset."

"Today?" Bruno responded in surprise. "That's odd. Usually, they keep you in one of the kennel rooms first."

"What is this room?" Haru asked. "Why do they call it Death Dungeon?"

Bruno gave Haru a pitying expression. "Because no dog has come out of here alive."

Haru immediately thought of the little white cat's words. *Animals go in, but they never come back out.*

"Oh no," Haru breathed. "What are they going to do to us?"

"They stick you with a needle and see how long it takes you to die," the German shepherd cut in.

"It don't take long at all," the Doberman said.

The two dogs roared with laughter again. That seemed to be the last straw for the Irish setter, who started howling and barking nonstop. Even when humans with hot sticks prodded him, he wouldn't stop howling, until he eventually collapsed. This was too much for even the Doberman and German shepherd, who both retreated to the back of their cages and curled up into tight, silent balls.

Haru watched horrified as the Irish setter twitched and foamed at the mouth. Then he went limp.

"Is he dead?" Haru asked Bruno.

Bruno didn't even look over. "In here, we are all dead," he said.

Haru whimpered, chilled to the bone. *I have to return home. Luke needs me.*

CHAPTER 11

LUKE SUFFERED A sleepless night filled with worry, fear, heartache, and the pain of missing his best friend. He felt sick to his stomach. But how could he care about himself when Haru must be feeling so scared and betrayed? Luke sat up in bed and stared at the space next to him where Haru should have been. The emptiness was severe. It felt as if he was missing a limb, or a piece of his heart. Suddenly, overwhelmed with fury, Luke began to hit himself on the head as he cried angry tears.

"It's all my fault! I shouldn't have said anything! I should have stayed in the back! This is all my fault!" He yanked at his hair viciously as he rocked back and forth.

The door to his room opened and his mother rushed in to grab hold of his hands and pull him into a tight embrace.

"It's not your fault, honey," she said. "You did nothing wrong."

"But it was because of me! I should've just stayed away! Haru would still be with me then!"

"You don't know that, Luke," his mom replied. "Nobody can predict what happens in life. You did nothing wrong. And we'll get Haru home again."

"Mom, Haru is family. He's my family," Luke cried brokenly. "I need him."

"I know, honey."

Haru barely slept all night, too anxious and scared to relax. He was the only one awake when the Irish setter was taken away, unmoving.

"Take this one back, he's too weak for our needs," the lead man said to Haru's kidnappers. "I'm glad you brought the new dog. We start with the new formula tomorrow and only the strongest and healthiest dogs will make it past the first course of radiation. Let's hope he's strong enough to survive the entire trial."

"If he does, we get a bonus, right?" Jim asked.

"Yes, a big one," the lead man agreed. "If he doesn't, then you'll go out and find more dogs."

Haru watched as they carried the unconscious animal out of the room. He wondered what would happen to the Irish setter now. But he knew the dog was lucky to be free of the dungeon.

A few hours later, one of the bad men who had kidnapped him returned with a cart of bowls of food and water.

"Good morning, you filthy animals," Stan said. Pulling out the tray under the door in front of each cage, he placed the bowls in and slid them shut.

"Eat up, big guy! You gotta have all your strength. Tomorrow is a big day for you." Stan pointed at Haru. "You're gonna do your part for the greater good! Ain't you special."

Stan sniggered as he slammed his fist on top of the cage and walked away.

The other dogs erupted into angry barking, but Haru was silent. He recognized the word "special." He was told he was special all the time and he knew it was a good thing. But the way the bad man had said it scared him. Today, he didn't want to be special.

The others stopped barking and began to eat their food hungrily, but Haru couldn't. He wasn't hungry. He looked over and saw Bruno wasn't eating either.

"You should eat, young one," Bruno said to him. "You'll need your strength."

"Why?" Haru asked bitterly. "They're going to kill us all anyway."

"If there's any chance of survival, you need to be strong," Bruno said. "Here only the strongest survive."

"What about you?" Haru asked. "Why aren't you eating?"

"It's too late for me," Bruno said. "I'm old and tired. But you are still young."

Haru stared at Bruno and saw the defeat etched into his posture. Haru could not give up. He had to return to Luke. Luke needed him.

I am young and strong, and if there's any chance of escaping, I must take it.

"Has any dog ever managed to escape from here?" Haru asked hopefully.

"No," Bruno sighed. "Escape is impossible."

Nothing is impossible for Haru. Luke's laughing voice echoed in Haru's ears. He remembered how Luke had taught him so many tricks. Things that other humans would say were impossible. To Haru, the word "impossible" always meant he would try anyway. Because that was how he was taught. So if there was a chance to escape this bad place, he would need to be ready to take it and make it possible.

Emboldened by the hope that now burned within him, Haru quickly wolfed down his food and drank his water. The meal cleared his mind a little and helped him think.

"Yes, I must escape so I can go home to Luke," he whispered. He began to repeat it to himself. It became his mantra. His mission. He would do whatever it took to be with his human.

CHAPTER 12

BY THE END of the day, Luke and his father had driven all over Virginia visiting animal shelters looking for Haru. But everywhere they went, he wasn't there. At the store, Mrs. Cole was waiting with Ben and Max. She shook her head sadly.

"No luck for us either. I have no idea where he could be. It's as if he's vanished."

At that moment, Luke knew with absolute certainty that Haru was at the factory and in danger.

"He didn't vanish, he's at the factory," Luke said urgently. "They're doing some kind of illegal testing on dogs. That's why we heard all that barking there. That's where Haru has to be."

"Luke, I filed a police report with Officer Blake, and he

is looking into the animal control men that took Haru," Peter explained. "He'll find out where they took him."

"It's not fast enough!" Luke cried out. "Please, Mrs. Cole, you need to look into it sooner! Before something terrible happens to Haru!"

Mrs. Cole stared at him in consternation. "I haven't had a chance to investigate the factory because my editor forced me to drop the story, but let me call some people."

"We have to find a way to get in and find Haru," Luke pleaded.

"I'll try my best, Luke."

Mrs. Cole took out her phone and immediately started calling her contacts.

As she talked, Ben and Max pulled Luke aside.

"I think Luke's right. Haru has to be at the factory," Max whispered. "We should go look for him."

Ben nodded. "Let's go to the factory tonight. If we find evidence, then they'll have to listen to us."

Luke nodded grimly. "Tonight."

By nightfall, Haru was exhausted. The bad men had taken him out of the cage many times to prick him with the SHOTS and examine his teeth, his eyes, and every part of his body. It was worse than any visit he'd ever had at the VETS. The last time, they took him to a strange-looking machine and the SHOTS that they gave him were so long and terrible that Haru had howled in anguish. He'd never felt such a burning pain in his life. It was so bad he vomited and dry heaved for a long time.

He desperately wanted to go home. To lie in Luke's comfortable bed. But here, he laid his tired, aching body on the hard metal surface of his prison. There was no comfort to be had. He shivered and cried. And he vowed that if he were to ever return to his family, he would never attack the mean woman ever again.

Late into the night, Luke waited until his parents were fast asleep. At 1:00 a.m. he texted his friends.

Luke: ready

Ben: k meet you at corner

Luke: k

Max: bring flashlight

Max: small shovel

Luke: shovel?

Max: you'll see

Sneaking carefully out of the house, Luke grabbed a garden shovel from the back storage room. He threw it into his backpack, put on his helmet, grabbed his bike, and rode down to the main road. The dim streetlights left small pools of light on the pavement as Luke pedaled hard. Several minutes later, he could make out the figures of two boys on bikes on the corner of Main and Kensington.

When he reached them, they both began pedaling. No words were exchanged. They all knew they shouldn't be out this late at night, going to a factory that was prohibited to the public. But they all loved Haru. They had to save him.

Within fifteen minutes, the boys were close to the lake and Max broke the silence.

"You brought a shovel, right?"

Luke nodded. "But what's it for?"

"The gate is locked," Max answered. "However, last time we were there, I noticed parts of the fence had lifted a little off the ground. We can dig a trench and slide under."

"Brilliant, Max!"

"I have my moments," Max replied with a grin.

They rode down to the lake and left their bikes by the side of the road. Walking swiftly but silently to the same fence where they'd seen the men in hazmat suits, the boys stopped and opened their bags.

Max started gagging. "The smell is even worse than last time," he whispered.

"Here, put on these masks." Luke pulled out three sealed N95 face masks. "I don't know how safe these will keep us from whatever's in there, but they're better than nothing. And it might help with the smell."

Max put on his mask and shook his head. "I can still smell it! That stink is the worst!"

Luke and Ben put on their masks and began looking for a good place to dig.

"Let's dig here," Max said, pointing to where the bottom of the fence was lifting and curling away from the ground.

The soil was loose and it took only ten minutes for them to finish digging a shallow trench. Luke slid under first and waited for his friends. Using their flashlights, they headed for the staircase they'd seen the men take last time. They crept down to the bottom level and found themselves standing in front of a locked metal door.

Luke put his ear to the door but couldn't hear anything. He shook his head. They went back up the staircase and started to creep alongside the building, looking for a way inside. It wasn't until they reached the back of the building that they found a small loading dock and a sliver of light from a door. They hurried to the door and found it slightly ajar. Sneaking inside, they found themselves in a dimly lit storage area. Luke turned to his friend and pressed a finger to his mouth for silence, then made a *follow me* signal. Slouching low, he slid farther into the storage room and immediately ducked behind a tall shelving unit. He could sense his friends right behind him as he slowly navigated around the shelves.

On the other side of the room, there was a set of double doors. Luke cracked one open and peered out into a hallway. It was empty, but they all heard the barking of dogs.

"Haru," Luke breathed. He opened the door wide and started running down the hallway. Only when Ben and Max caught up to him did Luke realize how dangerous this was.

"Luke, be careful," Ben whispered.

Just at that moment, they heard voices approaching. For a brief second, the boys froze in place. But then Luke spotted a door to his right. Seizing the handle, he pushed it open and they all jumped into a dark office. Leaving the door slightly ajar, Luke watched as two men in lab coats appeared at the end of the hall and stopped, finishing their conversation.

"Sinclair's getting really impatient. He's threatened to cut off our funding and fire everyone if we don't show results fast," the shorter man said.

"That old man needs to calm down! What does he think we're doing? Making blenders?" the other man's voice spluttered. "We're making history here! That takes time and patience."

"Well, the old man doesn't have a lot of either," the first voice said. "The idea of a youth serum isn't much use to him if he's dead."

"It isn't any good if it kills him also!"

"Yes, Dr. Hawley, but you haven't made any progress these past two years either!"

"What are you talking about, Graham? We've made lots of progress! We were able to create rapermidine! That was a huge breakthrough."

The first voice sighed. "Sure. For the makeup industry. The first miracle cream that actually reverses aging skin. Sinclair thanks you for his dewy complexion. But what he wants is an actual age-reversing youth serum that extends life, not just skin-care products."

Dr. Hawley laughed. "We're using the rapermidine with the radiopharmaceuticals in genome editing, which will target the aging gene and destroy it without harming anything else. That's why I needed the Z-forzyne. If we don't age, then we are forever young."

"In theory. But it hasn't worked for you yet. Your test subjects have all developed tumors and died from the excessive radioactivity," Graham responded.

"That's why we switched to dogs. They're not as delicate."

"And a hundred are dead."

"We are so close! The necropsy report shows that we would have been successful but for the tumors. This formula will work with the new radiation treatment to keep the tumors from forming. Once we have some successful trial runs, we can move to human subjects."

"Let's hope so. For your sake. We are running out of time and money."

As the scientists out in the hall began to walk away, Max bumped into a desk, sending a pile of paper crashing to the ground.

"What was that?" Dr. Hawley asked sharply.

The boys quickly hid behind the desk as footsteps approached the room. The door was thrown open. Through a sliver between two slats of wood in the corner of the desk,

Luke could see the two men silhouetted against the light. The tall scientist stepped into the room when a cell phone rang loudly. He stopped to answer his phone.

"What? Right now? Okay."

He turned to face the shorter scientist. "Speak of the devil. Sinclair is here and wants to see me immediately. As if I wasn't busy enough."

"Just reassure him that everything is on schedule," the short scientist responded.

"I know what I'm doing," Hawley snapped. Pointing at the door, he said, "Lock this door and fire Peterson. He can't remember to keep this door locked when I've reminded him that no one should have access to this room." The door slammed shut and Luke could hear the beep of the electronic keypad and then the click of the deadbolt. They waited until the footsteps could no longer be heard.

Max ran to the door. "This door locks on both sides. We need the passcode to get out," he said. "What do we do?"

Ben swept his flashlight all around the room. It was a large room with several desks and filing cabinets. Boxes of supplies and piles of papers cluttered the tables. In the back of the room, there was a set of windows with the blinds drawn. Ben and Max rushed over to try and open them. But Luke stood still, staring at all the papers on the desk and floor.

"Why would they lock this room?" Luke wondered out loud.

"Come on, Luke, let's get out of here," Ben whispered. He and Max had pushed open a window.

"Wait a minute," Luke said. He knelt down and began to pick up the documents. He held his flashlight to a page that seemed to be a data log for specimen number 137 with lots of dates and data. The last lines caused Luke to gasp in horror.

NECROPSY REPORT
Cause of death: sudden, intense growth of large malignant tumors

Reaching down, Luke grabbed another document. Another specimen with the same cause of death. Picking up more papers, Luke saw that they were all about animals that had been tested on. All died of tumors. Fear and fury sent a shudder through Luke's body as he grabbed as many papers as he could and shoved them into his backpack.

"What are you doing?" Max asked.

Luke closed his bag and stood up. "Evidence," he replied grimly. "Let's go."

Carefully sneaking out the window, the friends crawled under the fence and ran back to their bikes.

"So, what did you find?" Ben asked.

"The proof of what we overheard," Luke said. He pulled out one document and showed it to Ben and Max. "They gotta believe us now, right? Haru has to be here. We have to save him before they do any more illegal experiments."

Ben and Max nodded.

"Let's show this to Mom right away," Ben said.

"We gotta save Haru!" Max said.

As the boys biked off, a small white cat crawled out from the tall grass and peered after them.

"Oh no," Penelope whispered. "Haru is in the bad place?"

CHAPTER 13

BY THE TIME they reached the Coles' house, it was 3:00 a.m. and Mr. and Mrs. Cole were not happy with any of them. Until they saw the documents.

Mrs. Cole jumped to her feet and began pacing back and forth in the living room as she called her editor.

"Vance! We got him this time! I've got documents proving that Sinclair Industries has been doing illegal animal testing secretly at their laboratory!"

"How did you get them?"

Everyone could hear the editor's loud, excited voice through the cell phone.

"I can't reveal my sources, you know that," she replied, winking at the boys.

"Is it going to hold up in court?"

"I think so."

"I can't go by that; get it to our lawyers first thing in the morning," the editor said. "And then we'll talk!"

Hanging up the phone, Mrs. Cole hugged all the boys, giving an extra-long one to Luke.

"I'm going to put my entire report together and run it by our lawyers first thing this morning," she said. "And then I'll take it to the sheriff and hopefully we can get Haru out."

"Thank you, Mrs. Cole," Luke said.

"Don't thank me yet! The sheriff is going to have to get a court order first, and we know how hard it's been to get those against Sinclair," Mrs. Cole said grimly. "Now all of you go to bed. Luke, I'll tell your folks you're here."

Penelope slipped through the fencing of the bad place and circled the building. It was disturbing to see Haru's human Luke here. While Penelope didn't trust humans, she had come to form a bond with Luke and his family. She thought if she were to ever domesticate again, she wouldn't mind being with them. In large part because of Haru. He was unlike most animals she came across. Most abandoned pets were cautious and distrustful. The few dogs she did meet aggressively protected their homes and were more interested in chasing her off than making friends. Haru was sweet and caring and filled with a happy nature that was endearing. She really liked Haru and didn't want anything bad to happen to him. Which was why she was here, in a place she'd vowed never to return to, looking for Haru. For a little cat could poke her nose into places humans couldn't.

Hearing a noise, she slipped behind a garbage bin and watched as humans in shiny suits exited the building. She followed them to the far side of the compound, where she found other humans digging in the ground. A shudder coursed through her body. The humans were digging another grave for more dead animals. She just hoped it wouldn't be Haru.

Inside the bad place, Haru didn't know if it was evening or morning. There was no sunlight. No way to know what was happening in the outside world. The only way to mark time was when the bad men came to feed them and clean their cages or take them for testing. They'd dragged him over to the bright place for more of the SHOTS that made him feel like his insides were on fire. He didn't know how much more of it he could take.

"Good morning, you filthy animals!"

Haru opened his eyes as food and water was once again pushed into his cage. Dragging his tired body over to the bowls, he slowly ate, repeating his mantra. *I must escape so I can go home to Luke.*

"You okay over there, young one?" Bruno asked.

"I don't feel too good, Bruno," Haru replied. "What's going to happen to me?"

"You'll be okay," Bruno answered softly. "You'll get out of here. Don't worry."

"I hope so," Haru said. "I really need to get back to Luke."

Sleepy again, Haru slumped down on the floor and closed his eyes.

"I'm sorry, kid," Bruno whispered. "It's almost over and then you will rest forever."

Mrs. Cole woke Luke when his father came to pick him up in the morning. Ben and Max were still fast asleep and barely moved in their sleeping bags as Luke stepped over them. He followed Mrs. Cole outside, where his father and Mr. Cole were talking seriously.

"Luke, I'm very disappointed in you," Peter said. "I understand how much you love Haru, but you can't put yourself and your friends in danger."

"I'm sorry, Dad," Luke whispered. "I just miss him so much."

His father hugged him tight. "I know. But if anything happened to you, your mother and I would be destroyed. Especially your mother. She has never gotten over losing Jia."

Guilt wracked Luke as he remembered how devastated his mother was at his baby's sister's death. It was when he was five years old. They'd all been so excited to welcome Jia to the family. But she'd been born premature and had to stay in the hospital in an incubator. Luke only saw her once before she passed away. He barely remembered what she looked like, but he could never forget how sad his mother was. It took months for her to come out of her room. And while she was much better now, there were still some days when she would take out Jia's memory box and cry over the baby clothes and lock of baby hair for hours.

Mrs. Cole ruffled Luke's hair. "I'm going to the lawyers as soon as they call me. Don't worry, Luke. We'll get Haru back."

Mr. Cole, a man of very few words, patted Luke reassuringly on the back.

Hopeful for the first time in days, Luke nodded and climbed into his car while his father loaded Luke's bike in the trunk. Pulling out his phone, he looked at the photo of Haru on his lockscreen and let out a shuddering sigh.

"Haru, hang in there," he whispered. "I'll find you soon. I promise."

CHAPTER 14

HARU WAS VIOLENTLY awakened when the bad men seized him by the neck and dragged him from his cage.

"Today's your big day," Stan chuckled. "You need to do us proud or we don't get our bonus. And then your big day will be the worst day of your life."

The bad man put a choker and a leash on him and forced him into a walk. Still sick from all the SHOTS they'd given him, Haru staggered after the man. His brain still groggy from sleep and pain, Haru tried to look around for a way to escape, but they were going farther into the cavernous room and away from the exits.

At the far end of the laboratory, they passed the large clear boxes connected with wires located on high platforms, and several humans in shiny suits working on machines.

One of them pointed toward a nearby door where people in white coats and glasses were working. The glass door opened and Haru was led inside. Here, the people were not covered from head to toe and Haru could see their faces.

However, Haru recognized the voice of the tall evil man that he'd met the first time he'd come to the lab. He came over and began to roughly inspect Haru.

"He's not as strong as you promised me," the tall man said. "He's looking really sickly from the second set of injections. If he doesn't make it through the radiation treatment, it will be a complete waste of the formula."

"Oh, he'll make it," Jim bragged. "He's a tough one. The other dogs couldn't even walk after the injections."

"True," the scientist replied. "Let's see how long he lasts."

"I would like to see the specimen," an oily, low voice interrupted. The voice sent a shudder through Haru as he shut his eyes tight. He knew whoever this person was, he would not like them.

A rough hand grabbed Haru by the mouth and jerked his head up. Haru opened his eyes to see an old man with very dark hair and white eyebrows frowning at him. Cloudy brown eyes stared malevolently at him.

"This is the one you sent over, correct, dear cousin?"

Another face came into Haru's view. As sick as he was, Haru still growled and barked furiously at the sight of the mean woman from the store.

"Yes, I did," Mrs. Sinclair-Greene smirked. "I've always

hated this dog. Tried to poison him the first time I saw him, but he survived. He's always been repulsively healthy. Which makes him perfect for you."

"I was going to say he didn't look very healthy, but seeing you definitely gave that dog a burst of energy," the old man chuckled.

Mrs. Sinclair-Greene snapped her fingers at Stan. "You there, shut him up already."

Stan showed the hot stick, which quieted Haru into a whimper.

"There, much better," Mrs. Sinclair-Greene sighed. "I could hardly think before."

Behind the old man and mean woman, the tall scientist grimaced and stepped forward. "Why don't you both have a seat now as we are ready to begin the procedure."

Other people rushed over to lead the two old humans to seats in front of the glass wall next to a small table full of drinks and food.

"You'd better not disappoint me today, Hawley," old man Sinclair said.

Anger oozed from the tall man named Hawley. Without another word, he pulled on his shiny suit, fastened his headgear, and seized Haru's leash.

"Let's begin," he announced as he led Haru to the glass observation room and toward the testing area.

When they reached a bright glass case, Haru balked. Something told him that this was bad. Fighting the Hawley man, Haru struggled fiercely until the burning prod of the hot stick nearly made him faint. Even against the pain, he struggled mightily. But to no avail. Soon he was locked inside the glass case. It was so bright that he couldn't see anything outside the four walls of his prison. Metal arms came out from the floor of the box and clamped onto his legs and neck, gripping him in place. Another one of the SHOTS came from above his head. The huge needle inserted into his hindquarters, causing him to howl in pain. Haru wanted to collapse onto the floor, but the metal arms kept him standing. Suddenly, four large circular mechanisms with glass eyes descended from the ceiling. Beams of light shot out of the glass eyes in a coordinated pulsing. The beams didn't hurt Haru, but he felt sicker than before. His insides churned and he vomited his food again. His head hurt so much. Haru's whole body shook with pain.

What are they doing to me? When will it stop? Please make the pain stop.

The pain intensified and the noise in his head grew so loud he couldn't hear himself think.

Please stop. Stop. Stop.

Haru retched and retched but nothing came up. He was choking on nothing but air.

Luke. I need to escape and find Luke. Luke. Luke. Help me. Please.

And then it stopped.

"Dang it! He didn't make it? Shoot, there goes our bonus," Stan was muttering to himself.

Dr. Hawley slammed his fist on the counter, causing everyone to jump. "We don't have time for these setbacks! Prepare the remaining three for testing tomorrow. And get rid of this one."

Pivoting, Dr. Hawley stomped into the observation room where Mr. Sinclair and his cousin were getting ready to leave. They could hear the scientist apologizing profusely as he entered the room.

"That old geezer don't look too happy," Stan snorted. "I think the doc's in trouble."

Jim looked at Stan and shoved him. "You ain't paid to think, you're paid to do what he said. Now you heard him, get rid of that dog."

Mumbling angrily to himself, Stan put Haru's still body on a cart and pushed him out of the lab.

As Haru was rolled past the other dogs, Bruno let out a mournful howl that triggered the other two. A sad tribute to a lost life.

"Noisy jerks," Stan spat as he left the laboratory. He took Haru down a long corridor and to an elevator that transported them up to the ground floor. At the outside door, Stan pulled out a black body bag and stuffed Haru into it. He then pushed the cart away from the laboratory building toward the far side of the compound, rolling it through a mix of grass and gravel until he reached a large, deep trench.

"Good riddance, ya filthy animal," Stan muttered as he threw Haru's body bag into the trench. Without a backward look, he returned to the laboratory building.

From the bushes near the fencing, a small white cat stared intently after the man. Seeing Luke and his friends at the bad place had been shocking. Penelope had been too worried to leave. She'd decided to stick around to see if she could find Haru. It was the least she could do.

She made a quick decision to follow the man and swiftly caught up with him. Fortunately, the man was so suited up he never noticed Penelope walking right at his feet. She snuck into the building as he struggled to push the cart inside. In the hallway, Penelope followed the man closely until he opened the laboratory doors. She darted in and immediately hid behind a large pile of boxes.

CHAPTER 15

IT TOOK ALL morning for Mrs. Cole to clear her news story with the legal team and finally get it released on the *Virginia Central*'s website. It was splashed as breaking news on its home page and sent out as a news alert to all its subscribers. Within minutes it was picked up by major news outlets and became the number-one trending news item in the country.

Not only did the article raise the issue of illegal animal testing, but it suggested that there was a correlation to the fire and the widespread environmental pollution it had caused. Given the radioactive material used in the illegal testing, Mrs. Cole wrote that there should be more analysis of the pollution and that Sinclair should be held criminally liable.

The local news stations sent their camera teams to the factory and people were clamoring for a police investigation. By 3:00 p.m., groups of animal rights protestors as well as journalists were camped out in front of the factory compound.

Luke was over at the Coles' house, where Mrs. Cole was explaining that this was all good news. "They're going to have to stop any animal testing they are doing and face a criminal investigation," she said. "If Haru is there, we'll get him back soon."

Breathing an uneasy sigh, Luke prayed that it wouldn't all be too late.

In the trench, there was a sudden twitch of a body bag. A clawing sound. Then a slow but steady rip that tore the length of the bag. A dog burst out of the confines of its prison. For a long moment the dog stood frozen in place, disoriented. His brain was sluggish. He didn't know where he was or who he was. He only knew he had to move. He had to escape. First, climb out of the trench. Once on level ground, a sensation of danger sent caution signals through his brain. He slowly turned his head and saw the building. The sense of urgency and fear triggered his flight reflex.

Run away.

Danger.

Turning away from the building, he came to a fence. A strong compulsion sent him climbing over and leaping down to the other side. Once free of the compound, the dog began to run until he was deep into the woods. He then stopped to think.

The sense of danger was not as urgent now. But where was he supposed to go? Why was he in that cramped dark space? Why couldn't he remember anything beyond the moment he ripped open that bag he'd been in? So many questions. He paced back and forth for several minutes, trying to shake off the strange sensation that overwhelmed him. He felt as if he had forgotten something very important, but he just didn't know what it was. It bothered him and gave him a vague sense of discomfort and sorrow. If only he could remember.

Inside the bad place, Penelope had crept behind boxes and desks until she was positioned across from the dog crates. Craning her neck, she could see three dogs. But none of them were Haru.

"He must be in another room," she sighed. Before she could try to leave, someone familiar to her entered the room.

It was the boss man of the bad place who Penelope had mentioned to Haru. He stormed in, along with an angry-looking old woman.

"Where's Hawley?" he yelled.

A tall man in a silver suit came rushing over.

"Mr. Sinclair, Mrs. Sinclair-Greene, you shouldn't be in here without your protective gear . . ."

"I don't give a hoot about the radiation," Sinclair shouted. "I spent a bloody fortune bankrolling your experiments, not to mention half a million for a few grams of Z-forzyne! And I've nothing to show for it except some miracle skin cream that won't do a thing for me when I'm dead!"

"Sir, this new formulation should have worked, but that last dog was too weak. We've been preparing the new subjects for tomorrow, but there are news reporters and animal rights activists at the front gate! We're going to have to shut everything down and get rid of the evidence before they send federal investigators in here," Hawley responded.

"No, you're going to finish it now," Sinclair shouted. "Nobody is coming in here without my permission. My men will keep them all out. So finish it!"

Hawley nodded and urged the old couple into the observation room.

Dr. Hawley turned to the others in the laboratory. "Prepare the last three dogs for testing!"

"Dr. Hawley, they only just now received the first dosages. They won't be ready until tomorrow," one of the scientists interjected.

"Prepare them now! And increase the intensity of the beams twofold!"

"But that might kill them outright!"

"Then we'll study their corpses! Now get started."

From her hiding place, Penelope watched the flurry of movement in the laboratory. She stared intently when the humans dragged all three dogs to the back. While she was glad to see that none were Haru, it was frightening to see how poorly the dogs were being treated. They barked savagely and whined in pain as they were placed in three separate large, clear cases. Morbid curiosity propelled Penelope to crawl closer to see what was happening.

Bright lights pulsed as the dogs howled and cried in pain. Their bodies steamed as if they were being baked, and large lumps began to form on their faces and torsos. Horrified by the spectacle, Penelope closed her eyes tight but couldn't shut out their howls, which became louder and louder—until sudden silence ended the light show.

Shaking in fear, Penelope opened her eyes to see the unmoving forms collapsed at the bottom of each case. She watched as the tall human, Hawley, ripped off his headgear and screamed in anger. He began berating the other humans and throwing things. From the observation room, Sinclair and the Greene woman approached the scientist. Sinclair was visibly angry, while his cousin wore an expression of utter disdain.

"Once again you are a profound disappointment, Hawley," Sinclair said menacingly. "I'm going to destroy you. You will never work in this field again."

"Shut up, old man! It would have worked if you hadn't rushed me so incessantly!" Hawley screamed at Sinclair.

As the two men shouted at each other, a dreadful fear

and a terrible anxiety filled all of Penelope's senses. There was an electricity in the air, a heaviness that made her shudder. Her eyes were drawn to the body in the closest glass case. As she stared fixedly, she caught when the body began to twitch and shake. Penelope's eyes widened as she realized the immediate danger when it abruptly lurched to its feet. The creature standing inside of the box bore almost no resemblance to the dog that it had once been. Most of the fur had fallen off its body, leaving pinkish-red scarred skin stretched tight over massive lumps that distorted its face, limbs, and torso. It looked like a monster.

The humans were so engrossed in their hysterical fighting that they didn't notice what was happening until the creature began to growl and snarl loudly. It snapped the metal arms that had constrained it as if they were toothpicks. Behind it, the two other creatures rose to their feet.

Oh no, I have to get out of here! Penelope's hackles were raised. She instinctively knew that everyone in the building was suddenly in grave danger. Slowly she backed away, making herself as small as possible to evade notice.

Soon the other two dogs were snarling and barking viciously in their boxes and now had the complete attention of the humans. All the people in the laboratory began to gather closer, staring in fascination at the macabre scene before them. The creatures were grotesque and frightening. Penelope scrambled desperately for the exit, but it was closed. She pressed herself against the cold metal door and shivered in horror. Trapped in with the monstrosities.

"My experiment! It has succeeded! They're alive!" Dr. Hawley shouted.

Mrs. Sinclair-Greene drew back, revolted. "They're hideous!"

Meanwhile, Sinclair moved closer and peered with avid curiosity. "They're fascinating."

At that moment, the first dog shattered the glass and pounced on Sinclair. Pandemonium struck as the humans ran for the door and the two other dogs broke through their cases and attacked anyone within reach.

As soon as the door was flung open, Penelope streaked out of the laboratory and followed the humans escaping the building. Once outside, she flew across the pavement, ran to the crack in the fence that she'd entered through, and disappeared into the woods. She ran as far as she could before slowing down. She'd never been so scared in her life. She didn't know what was wrong with those dogs, but they'd come back from the dead as monsters. Whatever the bad humans had done to the dogs was truly evil. Penelope had sensed that their pure animal nature had been destroyed and what was left was a ravenous need to feed an endless emptiness. She'd never felt such a raw, intense hunger emanate from another creature. Their desire to kill and destroy, all driven by the loss of their essence. It was more than frightening. It felt like the end of the world. If those creatures escaped, no one would be safe.

As she ran through the forest, she sensed a familiar presence. Halting, Penelope sniffed the air and then changed course, searching, until finally she came upon a familiar figure staring up at the sky. Wild joy and a desperate relief surged through Penelope's thoughts.

"Haru? Is that you?"

The woods were not as confusing to the dog. Almost as if he knew them. He'd walked for a long time, mindlessly. His brain was still sluggish, but his body felt strong. He didn't know where he was going, but he felt that if he kept walking, he would find what he was looking for. This compulsion, this urgency, kept him moving. Whatever it was. A memory that was just out of reach and yet drove him forward.

Something had happened to him, but he couldn't remember what it was. There was a sense of profound loss that seemed to be the only emotion he could feel. He felt hollow. Empty inside. There was a desperate desire to fill the emptiness. With what, he didn't know.

A ray of light broke through the shadows of the trees in a beautiful shimmer. He stopped and stared up at the sky. Flashes of memory came in bits and pieces. The glass box. The metal leg restraints. Beams of pulsating light that made him sick to his stomach. Would this hurt him also? A shudder went through him. What had happened to him? Why did he feel so strange?

"Haru? Is that you?"

He recognized his name. *Haru.*

Immediately, visions of a boy overwhelmed him. He could hear his voice calling him.

Haru Haru, where are you?

"Haru, where've you been? Your human Luke has been so worried about you!"

Luke, his boy. The human boy was who he was looking for.

I must escape so I can go home to Luke.

Haru slowly turned. A small white cat approached him. Haru growled low in his throat. A sudden haze seemed to overwhelm him. An urge to kill rose within him as he focused on this intruder.

"I've been looking for you at the bad place," Penelope said as she came closer. "Because of your boy, Luke. He was also there trying to find you. That boy really loves you."

Haru stared at the cat as memories pushed back the dangerous haze that threatened his mind. He knew this cat. Her image melded with memories of finding her covered in gunk. Of humans cleaning her off. Of her telling him her name. A vision of his boy Luke cuddling the little cat. A small part of his brain cleared up. He remembered a name.

"Pe-nel-o-pe," he whispered.

"Yes! It's me! What happened to you? You look terrible. And your eyes! They look very different, very bright."

Penelope peered into Haru's face. "You need to go home to your family."

Home, Haru thought. *What is home?*

"I know this will hurt you to hear, but your boy, Luke, has been crying for you every day."

My boy, Luke. Once again memories sparked and flashed through his brain. Luke laughing, running, playing with him. Lying in bed together. Eating sandwiches. Chasing a ball. *Luke. My human boy. I have to get back to him.*

"Luke," he whispered. "I must escape so I can go home to Luke."

He lurched forward trying to find his way home, but his brain was malfunctioning, and he staggered in a circle. The sheer number of memories that flooded his mind overwhelmed him and left him shaking.

"Luke, I must go to Luke," he repeated.

"You're in bad shape," Penelope said. "Follow me, I'll take you home."

The cat ran ahead of him, and the urge to kill flooded his brain again. He snarled. His hackles rose as the red haze threatened to overtake him.

"You know the only reason I'm here is because I followed your boy," Penelope said over her shoulder. "He broke into the bad place trying to find you. That made me so worried. I kept thinking about all those poor dogs trapped there."

Her words stopped the confusion again. The red haze

receded as memories began to flood into his brain, clearing it of its sluggishness. Luke playing catch with him. Luke bathing him. Luke feeding him. Luke cuddling him.

Haru could feel his heart thumping in his chest painfully, as if it had been shocked awake. His mind raced, filled with so many visions. It was Luke who he had been trying to find. It was Luke he was heading to. He hadn't realized it, but instinct was taking him to his boy.

And to hear that his Luke had tried to find him in the bad place, had put himself in danger to look for him, was almost too much for him to process.

Haru shuddered. He remembered the cage. The fear. He remembered a voice that said, *In here, we are all dead.* But he didn't know who said it.

"So I snuck into the bad place looking for you, and I saw the most awful thing," Penelope continued, oblivious to her own danger. "I saw them experimenting on three dogs. They put them into these glass boxes and turned them into monsters that attacked the humans. I'm so glad you weren't in there!"

The bad place. The glass cases. The beams of light. The SHOTS that hurt more than anything he'd ever felt. The anguish and then the silence. The nothingness. Haru remembered it all. He froze in place.

"But I was there," he whispered. "Am I a monster too?"

Penelope loped back to his side, sniffing and studying him carefully. "There's something a little different about you, especially your eyes." she said. "You look like you suffered terribly."

"Yes," he responded slowly. "I did."

"Then let's get you back to Luke and your family," she replied kindly. "They'll take care of you."

Haru began to run again. "Luke," he sighed. "I'm coming home."

CHAPTER 16

ALL AFTERNOON LUKE, Ben, and Max watched the news anxiously. The crowd around the factory compound continued to grow. Mrs. Cole had even gone down there with a photographer. She called to say that she'd received word that federal investigators from the Food and Drug Administration (the FDA), the Centers for Disease Control and Prevention (the CDC), and the Environmental Protection Agency (the EPA) were all coming. But Sinclair had quadrupled the number of security guards around the compound, and they weren't letting anyone inside.

"Oh man, Sinclair is so screwed!" Ben gloated. "Mom is gonna get an award for her reporting."

Luke couldn't feel any satisfaction. Without Haru, he felt

like a part of him was missing. He wished he could be at the factory, but his parents said it wasn't safe. To take his mind off his sadness, his friends forced him to play video games.

A sudden breaking-news notification came over their phones.

They quickly turned on the TV news and saw footage by the local camera crew of people fleeing from the laboratory building. They were quickly rounded up by Sinclair security guards who shuttled them into vehicles.

Ben called his mother to ask what was happening, but she said she had no idea as no one was talking.

When Ben and Max's father called them to come home, Luke walked with them halfway, just to get out of the house.

"Don't worry, Luke, we're gonna get Haru back," Max was saying.

Luke nodded and waved goodbye. As he walked home, he worried about Haru. He tried not to think the worst. That they were too late. His mind couldn't even touch upon the mere idea of it. Haru had to be okay. He had to come home to him. Luke couldn't bear to think of any other possibility.

Reaching the store, Luke walked to the back and stared out into the woods. He wondered where Penelope was. He wished she would come visit him and cheer him up. As he sat on a tree stump, he caught the rustling of leaves in the woods up ahead.

Luke jumped to his feet and approached. "Penelope, is that you?" he called.

The noise stopped and then receded. Luke slumped back down on his stump.

Penelope blinked in shock as Haru backed away and slunk into the deep woods. Chasing after him, she found Haru leaning his head against a tree.

"What's the matter?" she asked. "Why aren't you going to your boy?"

Haru heaved a deep sigh. "I think there's something the matter with me," he said. "I feel strange, not myself. They did something to me, and now I keep having these violent urges."

Haru stared at Penelope in anguish. "But I promised that if I returned to Luke, I would never hurt another human again. So how can I return? What if I hurt Luke? I'm a monster!"

Penelope stared at Haru compassionately. "Did you have these urges with me?"

"Yes," Haru whispered.

"How did you stop them?"

"You're my friend."

"That means you can control them," Penelope said. "Haru, you are a good dog, not a monster. You would never hurt Luke or his family. And not returning to Luke is hurting him more."

"Do you really think so?" Haru asked hopefully.

"Yes, so go home."

Haru turned around to face home, but then stopped. "Not yet. Can you go first? I need to make sure I can control the monster they put in me."

Penelope deliberately rubbed herself against Haru's legs. "Okay, Haru, but don't take too long."

Haru followed the little cat as she returned to Luke's place. He felt hopeful for the first time since this terrible situation began. He did not feel the killing haze when she'd brushed against him. If anything, he remembered his affection for her. He remembered asking her to stay because she made Luke happy, even though his human mom was always sneezing and itchy around her. They all still wanted her to stay.

My family, he thought gratefully. *I promise I will return to you, Luke. Just wait a little longer.*

Haru stayed in the shadows as he watched Penelope bound toward his human boy.

"Penny!" Luke opened his arms and swept the little cat into a tight hug. "Thank you for coming back to me. I missed you. I miss Haru."

Luke wiped away tears as he cuddled Penelope to his chest.

Haru watched wistfully. He wanted so badly to join them.

"Just a little longer," he whispered. "I promise I'll return to you."

CHAPTER 17

LUKE WAS WATCHING the news coverage in the store while his parents worked. There were some customers shopping while a few regulars from the nearby gas station sat eating sandwiches. But everyone stopped to watch the developing news of the protests at the Sinclair factory. The animal rights activists were camped out in front of the factory, and the police were stationed around the fence to prevent them from trying to get in.

The security guards had locked down the buildings and had claimed that there was some kind of emergency going on inside. But nobody knew what was happening.

"They're gonna have to shut down that factory. I say good riddance," a grandfatherly customer said. "It's Sinclair's fault that we can't use the lake anymore. I hope he goes to jail!"

A woman nodded in agreement. "That factory has been nothing but a nuisance. And the Sinclairs are all awful people!"

"Man, I hate that Sinclair-Greene woman the most," Carlos Ramirez, the gas station mechanic and owner, said. "She's a real piece of work. Came into the shop the other day to tell us she's raising our rent again and then expects us to service her car for free."

Peter nodded grimly. "She's a terrible person."

"Peter, did she raise your rent also?"

Luke's father nodded. "I don't think we can afford to stay."

The mechanic sighed. "I hear you. I don't know if we can either."

After everyone left, Luke's parents sat him down for a family discussion.

"Luke, it may be time to move from this area," his dad said. "We can't afford the rent and business hasn't been great."

"We can move to New Jersey near your uncle John and aunt Virginia," his mom said. "You can see your cousins again and we can start over."

Luke bit his lip. "But I wouldn't see my friends anymore," he replied slowly.

His mother gave him a hug. "I'm so sorry we have to

put you in this difficult position, honey. I know how close you are to Ben and Max. I know how much you will miss them."

Blinking away hot tears, Luke dashed the back of his hand against his eyes. Ben and Max were his closest friends. He couldn't imagine not seeing them all the time.

"We wouldn't ask this of you if we had any other choices," his father said.

"I know," Luke replied. He took a deep breath. "But not until Haru comes back. I'm not leaving without him."

His parents exchanged a worried look. Before they could reply, Luke got a text message in his group chat.

Ben: mom says there are weird rumors at the factory

Luke: like what?

Ben: people hearing screaming and groaning

Max: ZOMBIES!!!!

Ben: lots of barking and growling

Max: REVENGE OF THE DOGS!!!

Ben: police went in over an hour ago

Ben: still not out

Luke: what's happening?

Max: MUTANTS!!!

Ben: shut up max

Max: you shut up

Luke: did anyone say anything about dogs?

Ben: people saw dogs running out of the building into the woods

Luke: Great!

Luke: I'm gonna go look for Haru

Ben: but luke there's something else

Luke: what

Ben: they said they looked like monsters

Max: what like mutants?

Ben: yeah like they'd been experimented on

Luke sucked in a deep breath before texting.

Luke: doesn't matter I'm gonna find him

"Mom, Dad, I'm going outside with Penny," he said, not looking them in the eye.

"Okay, son, don't go too far," his dad replied.

Luke nodded and headed to the back room. Penny wasn't there. Grabbing his flashlight, Luke walked out of the store to search for Haru.

CHAPTER 18

PENELOPE HAD GONE to check on Haru and found him acting oddly. He refused to look at her. Hunger had brought back the red haze, and he didn't want to hurt his friend.

"What's the matter?" she asked.

"I think I'm hungry," Haru replied.

"Ah," she said. "You need to learn to hunt. Watch and learn."

Penelope scoured the whole area, trying to find a scent. When she found what she was looking for, she became very still as her eyes locked on something in front of her. She stalked slowly forward, her movements barely discernible. Suddenly, she streaked out of the tall grass and pounced on an unsuspecting mouse. She brought it over still alive and held it by the tail in front of Haru's paws.

For a long moment, Haru stared at the frantic mouse, the desire to eat it growing within him. But its cries for help and its desperate struggle to free itself cut through his hunger. Luke would not like it if he hurt a living creature. Haru turned away with a shudder.

"I can't," he said. "Please just let it go."

Penelope released the mouse. Haru watched it streak into the safety of a tree.

"But aren't you hungry?" she asked curiously.

"I'll be fine," he replied. "I can control myself."

"How?"

"I think of Luke and what he would want me to do," Haru said. "And he'd be proud of me and make me a sandwich."

Haru took a deep sniff in and released it. "My favorite chicken sandwich with cheese."

Just talking about Luke chased off the remnants of strange violent urges that would come over him. It gave him relief and hope that he could rejoin Luke soon.

Thinking of Luke brought him vividly to mind again. Haru could hear his voice and smell his scent. The familiar scent of boy. His boy. Sighing, he closed his eyes and lay down on the grass. He inhaled deeply.

Haru's eyes opened wide and he jumped to his feet. Wait! He really was smelling Luke. What was Luke doing out in the woods? Didn't he know how dangerous it could be?

Haru raised his head and sniffed in a big circle before

charging ahead, looking for Luke, Penelope close on his heels.

"What is it?" she asked in alarm.

Not answering, Haru homed in on the scent and ran faster until he saw the beloved shape of his human roaming the woods. So happy to see him, Haru couldn't help himself. He let out a short whine. Luke turned around immediately. His face lit up with the biggest smile.

"Haru, it's really you! I can't believe it!" Luke ran to Haru's side and burst into tears as he hugged him tight. "I'm so sorry, Haru! It was all my fault! I won't let anyone take you from me ever again!"

Haru pressed his head against his boy's chest, listening to his strong heartbeat, and he felt at peace. The hollow within him dulled. This was what he needed. When Luke pulled away, Haru gazed up at him with trust and love until Luke gasped in shock.

"What happened to your eyes?" Luke put his hands around Haru's head and stared in shock at his eyes. "They're this weird blue! What did they do to you?"

A deep dread chilled Haru as he worried about what Luke would find. What he would think. He took a step back and looked down, feeling ashamed, not wanting Luke to see the changes to his body. But Luke just stepped closer and crooned soft words.

"It's okay, Haru, let me see," Luke whispered as he examined Haru's body. He gasped at finding bloody blisters, burns, and deep puncture wounds.

"Oh, Haru," he breathed as he hugged his dog tight once more. "I'll never let anyone hurt you again. Let's go home."

Haru let out a deep shuddering breath, releasing the fear and dread he'd been holding within. He'd been so afraid of being rejected, of no longer being good enough. But he knew now that Luke would always love him. With Luke, he was home.

A loud meow made them both turn around. Penelope extended her paws toward Luke and he immediately picked her up.

"Penny, were you the one who found Haru for me? You wonderful cat! You definitely deserve a ride," Luke said as he placed her on his shoulder.

They headed home, Haru walking as close as possible to Luke. Luke kept his hand on Haru's neck and Penelope clung to his shoulder. Haru listened happily as Luke chatted away. Hearing the voice he'd longed to hear more than any other. Hearing Luke say the words that meant so much to him. How much Luke had missed him and loved him. These words and Luke's presence completely filled the void that had previously formed within Haru.

As they approached the store, Haru halted at the flashing lights of the police car that had just pulled up. Luke stopped also, then led Haru through the back door and straight into the storage room where Penelope sometimes stayed. He took Haru to the nook and urged him to be quiet.

"Stay here, Haru. Let me see what the police want."

He put Penelope on a nearby pillow and left the room, closing the door firmly behind him.

Penny curled up next to Haru and yawned.

"How are you feeling now?"

"Tired and sleepy, but very happy," Haru answered. His eyes gleamed a pale blue in the dimly lit room. He closed his eyes and passed out hard.

Luke entered the main store and noticed the two police officers speaking with his parents at the counter. Worried that they might be there because of Haru, he walked over to the counter to eavesdrop on their conversation.

"We're going door-to-door to ask people to stay inside; there've been attacks by rabid dogs that have hospitalized a few people," the officer was saying. "If you see any of them, do not approach and call 911 right away."

Lydia looked alarmed and called out to Luke. "Did you hear that? You can't go outside today. It's too dangerous, okay?"

Knowing Haru was safe in the storage room, Luke nodded. He was glad he'd been cautious. The officers might have taken Haru away.

Loud static filled the air as the officer's walkie-talkie went off. Luke couldn't understand what was being said, but after receiving their message, the policemen both hurried out of the store. They drove off with their sirens blaring.

A nervous feeling settled in the pit of Luke's stomach. He pulled out his phone and looked at the group chat again.

"Zombies? Mutants? What the heck is going on?" Luke wondered.

"What did you say, honey?" his mom asked.

Shaking his head, Luke suddenly realized Haru must be hungry. "Mom, can you make me a turkey sandwich with cheese?"

He took the sandwich to the back room, along with some of Haru's special treats and some water. But Haru was completely passed out and didn't even budge.

"You sleep, Haru. I'll take care of you."

Luke grabbed the first aid kit and a clean, wet towel and began to gently wipe off the blood from Haru's fur. But when he went to disinfect the puncture wounds he'd seen earlier, they were no longer there.

"That's odd. I know I saw them," he said. He dug through the fur and peered at the skin until he found what looked like small healing puncture marks. Before, where he'd seen terrible burns, all that was left were small, smooth bald patches.

"How are you healing so fast?" Luke wondered. He stroked Haru's head and smiled as Haru opened his eyes. "I'm so glad you came back to me."

Luke stared into Haru's eyes to really take in the changes. Haru's normally hazel-brown eyes were now filled with bright blue flecks. The iris had a thick dark blue ring around it. Luke remembered noticing flecks of blue in Haru's eyes before, but now his eyes were mostly blue instead of light brown. They were intense and eerie.

Smelling the sandwich, Haru got up and nudged Luke's leg and then the plate.

Laughing, Luke handed him half at a time and watched as Haru wolfed it down in seconds. The terrible ache inside Luke's chest had finally dissipated. He felt like he could breathe again.

"I love you, Haru," Luke said as he buried his face in Haru's neck.

CHAPTER 19

LUKE WANTED TO tell his parents of Haru's return. But he worried that they would think there was something wrong with Haru, or that he had rabies. Luke didn't want to lose his best friend again. His parents were overly cautious, and Luke couldn't explain Haru's blue-ringed eyes or strange healing abilities. Though his mother didn't come to the storage room because of Penny, his father still did every night after they closed the deli. Luke had to get Haru out first.

"Okay, Haru, I know you want to stay with me, but we have to go to the shed for now because I can't lose you again. You have to hide, okay?"

Haru cocked his head. Luke knew Haru understood "hide." They used to play hide-and-seek all the time. And

Haru knew not to come out until Luke found him.

"Let's go," Luke whispered. "Penny, you can come keep Haru company."

Luke scooped up the little cat and led Haru from the rear door. The large backyard had a parking spot and a driveway that curved around the store and toward the road. Behind the parking spot, the lawn extended all the way to the woods that surrounded the entire expanse of the back. To the far right of the yard was a small shed that Luke's parents used for extra storage.

Outside, the clear sky had turned the pink and purple glory of a summer sunset. As they hurried across the backyard, Luke once again felt the nervous tingle in the pit of his stomach. His ears seemed weird, until he realized it was the unnatural silence that surrounded them. Next to him, Haru froze and growled. Even Penelope began to spit angrily.

Luke suddenly remembered the police officer's warning to stay inside just as he noticed the two dark shadows moving toward them from the woods. Horror filled him as he took in their grotesque forms. They were clearly once dogs, but whatever experiments they'd endured had mutated them into monsters. Luke could see from their remaining forms that one had been a German shepherd and the other a Doberman. But multiple large tumors were piled all over their completely hairless bodies and faces. They were snarling and slobbering, and their dark eyes were locked on Luke.

Haru shoved his body against Luke, urging him toward the shed. Luke launched himself at the door as the monster dogs surged forward. Gasping in fright, he pulled it open and turned to see Haru grab the Doberman by the neck and throw him at the German shepherd.

"Haru! Get in here!" Luke shouted.

For once, Haru didn't listen to Luke and instead slammed his body against the door, shutting Luke and Penny into the safety of the shed.

"No, Haru!"

Luke jumped to the window at the side of the door and watched as Haru fought off the monsters. But they were so much bigger and frightening. Putting Penny on a side table, Luke searched the shed for a weapon and locked eyes on a large shovel. Seizing it, Luke pushed open the door, ready to protect his best friend.

CHAPTER 20

THE MOMENT HARU had stepped outside, he sensed something was very wrong. The air was too still. Too quiet. But it had been too late to turn back when he finally realized what it was. The Doberman and the German shepherd from the laboratory. His cage mates. Haru smelled them before he saw them. They stank of death and scorched flesh and chemicals, a unique unpleasantness that reminded him of the bad place. When they'd finally appeared, they were unrecognizable, morphed into huge frightening versions of themselves. Their eyes looked completely dead, and yet the snarling, gaping mouths made clear that the danger was very real. Haru knew he had to protect Luke and Penny.

Once he'd placed himself between his human and the monsters, he assessed the threat and was surprised to note how sharp his senses were. His sense of smell and hearing and even his eyesight had never been so strong. It was almost as if he could feel the air moving around him. He was hypersensitive to every danger and his entire body had become electrified with the ability to protect his human. This same ability made him keenly aware of the creatures' intense focus on Luke. They didn't even seem to notice Haru. The drool that coursed incessantly down the sides of their mouths intensified as they stared at Luke. Haru could sense when they were getting ready to pounce. His mind completely attuned to their muscles contracting and then releasing. Instinctively, he'd pushed Luke hard toward the shed. Haru then pivoted to meet the threat head-on. The Doberman charged first. Haru seized him by the neck and threw him at the German shepherd, sending them both flying into a tree several feet away.

Haru could see Luke had opened the shed door and was ordering him to come inside. Without hesitation, Haru slammed the door shut and turned to face the monstrous dogs. He was shocked and grateful for his enhanced strength, but there was no time to think, as both creatures were back on their feet and circling him.

"What are you doing here? Leave this place!" Haru shouted.

Neither dog responded. Haru could see from their eyes that the violent killing haze he'd felt before had taken complete control of their minds.

Behind him, he heard the shed door open, and his heart sank to know that Luke was no longer safe inside.

"Get away from him!" Luke shouted, brandishing the shovel.

Alarm and fear for his boy threw Haru for a loop. He almost missed the first attack. With lightning speed, Haru put his head down and rammed into the German shepherd and then the Doberman, knocking both off their feet and sliding them ten feet into the brush. He hastily urged Luke back toward the store by pushing into him. But Luke refused to leave.

"Look out, Haru!" Luke waved his shovel desperately at the charging Doberman.

Haru rose onto his back legs and leapt onto the Doberman's back, pancaking the other dog to the ground, and kicked its head. Then he rammed into the German shepherd and shoved him past the shed and sent him soaring into a ditch. Racing back, he dragged the Doberman and sent him tumbling into the German shepherd that had staggered to its feet. Haru turned to see Luke still outside. He was frustrated that he couldn't tell Luke to go to safety when the German shepherd caught him in a surprise choke hold. Haru yelped in pain and struggled strenuously, managing to heave the other dog over his back so hard that its head smashed into a pile of rocks, knocking him out.

Haru staggered to his feet to help Luke and saw the Doberman stalking his boy. Before the Doberman could attack, a blur of white tangled into his feet, sending him tripping. Penny then scrambled up Luke's body and onto his shoulder. Luke raised the shovel high and brought it down hard on the dog's skull. Haru ran to Luke's side and forced him into the store and then stood guard outside, growling. He could hear Luke run inside, screaming for his parents' help.

Haru watched as the German shepherd and Doberman slowly got to their feet and locked their eyes on him. They snarled, exposing their sharp canines dripping with drool.

"Give us the boy," the Doberman growled.

"Yes, give him to us and we won't kill you," the German shepherd said.

"Never!" Haru shouted.

Their hackles rose as they prepared to attack. Then suddenly, they turned their heads to see another large figure approaching. Haru's eyes widened in shock as he took in the large, bulky black dog with droopy eyes rimmed in red and one huge lump on its back and half of its face. Haru recognized him immediately.

"Bruno, I'm so sorry," Haru barked.

At his words, the figure stopped as if confused.

"Bruno! It's me, Haru!"

"Ha-ru?" Bruno asked. "You—died?"

"Yes," Haru said. "But then I woke up again. What happened to all of you? Did they hurt you too?"

The red rings around Bruno's eyes glowed as he spoke.

"They put us in the same boxes, but they rushed the process far faster and made it much stronger. We watched them torture you and die. But what they did to us was far worse. Look what it did to our bodies. They turned us into monsters."

The other two dogs whined.

"Now you must join us to punish the humans," Bruno continued. "They did this to us! When we bite them, they die and come back as monsters. It is the perfect revenge!"

He growled and the other two dogs growled in unison.

"Not all humans are bad," Haru said. "This is my family. This is my home. I will protect them with my life. I would advise you to leave."

"Haru, you are either with us or you are the enemy," Bruno thundered.

Haru made himself as big and wide as possible, his fur standing on end. He snarled viciously. "Then we fight, and I will tear you all apart."

Bruno stilled. "Why?" he asked. "Why do you still protect them after all they have done to us?"

"The humans that hurt us are evil, I agree," Haru replied. "But not all of them are. You know this also, Bruno. Even though you are hurt and angry, you know there are humans that are good. And I will protect them. Because it was my love for my human family that kept the darkness at bay. The same darkness that I can see has gripped all of you. When I would have attacked and killed, the thought of my humans brought me back to myself."

The four dogs stood frozen in place for a long moment.

"I do not understand you, Haru. But I will honor your request this once only," Bruno said. "I hope we never cross paths again. For next time, we will destroy you." Bruno abruptly stormed off into the woods without a word. The other two dogs quickly followed suit.

Relieved, Haru watched the dogs disappear. He sniffed the air until he couldn't smell them anymore. Only then did he turn back to the door. On cue, the door opened, and Luke called him in.

CHAPTER 21

ONCE INSIDE, LUKE ran screaming for his parents.

"What is it? What happened?" his dad asked in alarm from behind the counter.

"There are monster dogs in the backyard!" Luke yelled. "They are attacking Haru! Please call the police!"

His mom clutched at her chest in fright. "Monster dogs? The ones that the police were talking about? With rabies?"

Peter immediately grabbed the phone and dialed the police. The phone kept ringing and ringing. "That's strange. Nobody is picking up."

"We have to help Haru!" Luke cried, pulling on his father's arm.

His mom grabbed Luke by his shoulders. "No, honey, you can't go out there! It's too dangerous."

"But Haru! He saved me from them! We have to save him!"

Peter kept dialing. "I can't get anyone on the phone." He slammed the phone down and grabbed the baseball bat he kept behind the counter for protection.

"Let's go help Haru," he said grimly.

Luke raced ahead, but before he could open the door, his father stopped him. "Let's check to see what is happening first."

Luke was agitated, but he leaned over to peer out the window and gasped. "They're gone! Haru is safe!"

He immediately opened the door and let Haru inside.

Luke's mother, who had come running over, took one look at Haru and gasped.

"What's wrong with his eyes?"

"Nothing," Luke retorted sharply. "He's fine."

Lydia moved slowly closer to Luke and swiftly pulled him behind her. Her eyes were fixated on Haru.

"Something's happened to Haru," she said slowly. "His eyes are unnaturally blue. And look at his back. His fur is falling out."

Luke pulled away from Lydia and went back to Haru's side.

"Mom, stop, there's nothing wrong with him."

"Nothing wrong yet," she said. "How do we know he won't change? They said the monster dogs were from the lab, where they'd been experimented on."

His father agreed, his expression serious. "We need to be cautious. Especially if he has rabies."

"He doesn't have rabies!"

"We don't know that for sure," his father replied.

Before Luke could respond, he heard Mrs. Cole yelling for his parents in a panicked voice from the front of the store.

"Peter! Lydia! This is an emergency! Peter! Lydia!"

Alarmed, Luke's parents exited the storage room, admonishing Haru to stay. Luke followed them.

Mrs. Cole was madly dashing around, grabbing water bottles and food and shoving them into a large canvas bag.

"Peter! Lydia! Pack some essentials and get in your car! We have to evacuate immediately!" Mrs. Cole shouted in a fearful voice. "Something terrible happened at the factory! Some kind of virus or mutation! Probably from the dogs that bit people. And those people died and then they suddenly came back to life. Dangerous and aggressive! And the infected people began attacking the protestors. I saw them change right in front of my eyes! Like zombies. They were zombies!"

"Patricia, you're not making any sense," Peter said.

"No, listen to me!" Mrs. Cole seized Peter by his arms and shook him hard. "If zombies are too hard to believe, think of what rabies does to the brain! How it causes animals to become aggressive and violent. That's what's happening! Some virus that's like rabies that's highly contagious. And when an infected person bites another, they transmit the virus immediately! I saw dozens of people turn rabid in minutes. It's a plague. Please, please, you have to listen to me! Get your things, get in the car, and get out!"

Luke ran to the front windows and saw Mr. Cole outside his car, brandishing a rifle, and Ben and Max seated inside, staring out the window with frightened expressions. They waved frantically when they saw him and pointed to their phones.

Luke realized he hadn't checked his phone in a long time. Pulling it out, he saw a stream of panicked, urgent texts from his friends.

Ben: LUKE YOU HAVE TO LEAVE NOW!

Max: its zombies theyre real!!!

Max: im scared

"Patricia! Let's go!" Mr. Cole yelled from outside.

Mrs. Cole pressed several large bills into Peter's hand and grabbed the bags of food. "You have to believe me and leave immediately. Please be careful!"

And then she bolted out of the store and into the car. Mr. Cole gave a grim nod to Luke's parents and drove off in a hurry. Luke stared at his friends' pale faces and wondered when he'd see them again.

CHAPTER 22

"MOM, DAD, WE gotta go now!"

Peter nodded. "Lydia, Luke, pack a small bag of your things. I'll grab food."

Luke raced upstairs with his mom, grabbed his backpack, and shoved a bunch of clothing and his prized comics in it. He could see his mom throwing clothes into duffel bags in her room. Snatching up an extra duffel, he raced downstairs to fill it with dog and cat food and treats. He then grabbed as many snacks as the bag would fit before returning to Haru and Penny, who were waiting patiently by the back door.

"Luke, get in the car!" his dad shouted from outside. He was filling the back of the SUV with water and boxes of food.

Luke picked up Penny and led Haru to the family SUV, but his father stopped him.

"I'm sorry, son, but Haru can't come with us. He's infected."

"No, he's not! He's fine!" Luke shouted.

His father ran a hand through his hair.

"I know you love Haru, but it's my job to put my family first."

"Haru is family! He's our family!" Luke was crying.

"No, I'm sorry," Peter said. He took Luke's bags, threw them in the back. Then he picked up a resisting Luke and put him in the car. "Haru, stay."

Luke was screaming and trying to unlock the door, but the childproof locks kept him inside. Penelope yowled in dismay as she stared at Haru through the window.

Luke's mom finally appeared and put her bags in the back. Peter rushed to the driver's seat and was putting on his seat belt when Lydia suddenly jumped out of the car.

"Honey, what are you doing?" Peter asked in shocked dismay.

"I forgot Jia's memory box," she yelled.

"Lydia, please, we have to go!"

"I can't leave my baby girl!" Lydia raced into the building.

Luke was sobbing as his father started the car and backed it up, ready to take off.

"Dad, please! I can't leave Haru!"

Peter didn't respond. Luke could see the sorrow and guilt

in his father's face, but he couldn't change his mind. He tried to crawl out the back of the car, but his dad seized him by his leg.

"Luke, I'm sorry, you're my son! I have to put my wife and child first," Peter said in an anguished voice.

Luke shook off his father and pressed his face to the window, screaming Haru's name.

Outside, Haru's attention was drawn away; he stared fixedly beyond the car. Luke could hear Haru's deep, loud growl. He could see Haru's head dip lower as he bared his teeth fiercely, and how dramatically his hackles raised, making Haru look even bigger. A chill shuddered through Luke's body as he looked to the other side of the car.

"Dad!" Luke screamed. A group of six infected people were walking toward the driver's side, their attention fixed on Luke and his father. If Luke's father had been skeptical about the idea of zombies, the sight approaching them would convince him. They were a mix of lab-coat-wearing scientists and security guards from Sinclair. One was missing his jaw, another an eye. They all showed signs of having suffered some kind of terrible animal attack. Luke was reminded of the three monster dogs he'd seen earlier. Were they responsible for what happened to these people? This wasn't rabies. These people looked dead. They looked like zombies.

"Oh no, Lydia!" his dad shouted in a panic.

Luke froze in horror. His mother was still in the store.

The infected reached the side of the car and began banging on it, rocking it side to side.

"Mom! Haru! Zombies!" Luke screamed.

Haru was once again confused. He didn't understand why his human dad was not letting him in the car. They wouldn't leave him, would they? It upset him so much to see Luke crying. Luke was trying to get out of the car, but Haru knew his human would be safer there. And then he saw his human mom run back to the house. Alarmed, Haru felt his hackles rise as he sensed an approaching danger. He growled fiercely. He had to warn his family to stay inside. Running to the front of the car, he watched as humans that smelled of the evil place staggered slowly from the woods and toward the vehicle. There was something very wrong with these people. They had the same stench of sickness and death as Bruno and the monster dogs. Haru realized that this was what Bruno had meant by revenge. His family was in terrible danger.

Haru was torn. He wanted to chase off the infected, but he knew he had to protect his human mom, who was still inside. He began to bark loudly, trying to scare off the approaching mob, but they ignored him. They were focused on Luke and his human dad inside the vehicle. They reached the car and began to bang on the windows.

Haru wanted to attack them, but at that moment, the back door slammed shut and they could all see Luke's mom exiting the building.

The sound drew the attention of the infected people as they slowly began to move toward her. Luke's dad threw the car into drive, ran over the two in front of his car, and then reversed and slammed some of the infected into the side of the building that protruded right behind them, crushing them against the brick wall. But the two in front got right back up and started bearing down on Luke's mom, who screamed in horror.

Haru heard Luke scream the word "zombies" again. Was that what these sickly people were? Zombies? Haru launched himself at the zombies, knocking them down like bowling pins. With unreal strength, Haru grabbed one infected by its lab coat and flung it all the way across the yard, where it smashed against the shed and crumpled. The jawless security guard zombie had stood up and lurched toward Lydia. Haru ran in a wide circle before lowering his head and ramming the guard into the air, sending it tumbling down the ditch.

By now, his human dad had reached his human mom's side and rushed her to the SUV. He threw the passenger-side door open and pushed her.

"Lydia, please! Get in! We have to get out of here!"

She threw herself into the car but stopped Peter from closing the door. She yelled, "Haru, come!"

Without hesitating, Haru jumped into the seat and climbed over the front console and into the back next to Luke. Lydia slammed the door and locked it, and Peter jumped in just as one of the zombies, pinned against the building, freed himself and banged on Luke's window.

"Peter, go!" Lydia screamed.

Throwing the car into drive, Peter peeled out of the driveway and onto the main road.

In the back seat, Luke was hugging his dog hard.

"Haru Haru," Luke cried into his dog's chest. Penelope snuggled close to both of them.

Haru closed his eyes and released a deep breath. His family had not been leaving him. They had needed him to save his human mom.

Peter was now driving down Route 1. Traffic was fairly light as he glanced at his wife in surprise.

"I thought you were worried about Haru being infected," Peter said cautiously.

Lydia looked back at where Haru was now settled into Luke's lap, his eyes closed.

"He's family," she replied. "Besides, you saw what those zombies looked like. Haru is still just Haru."

Peter stared at the scene in the back seat through his rear-view mirror. He sighed. "You did the right thing, honey," he said. "I'm sorry, Luke. I shouldn't have tried to leave Haru behind."

Luke glanced up to see the apology in his father's eyes. He nodded. "It's okay," he said. "Haru is here now, and we're never letting him go again. Promise me."

His dad and mom nodded and raised their pinkies. "Promise."

CHAPTER 23

THEY'D BEEN DRIVING for a long time when Luke fell asleep, his arms still wrapped tightly around his dog.

Penelope patted Haru's back as if to reassure herself he was actually there.

"I really thought they were going to leave you behind," she whispered.

"I was a little worried," he replied.

"But your human never doubted you, never stopped fighting for you."

"I know," Haru sighed. He cuddled closer to Luke. "He is my family."

Glancing over to Penelope, he said, "And now you are too."

"Yes, the woods are no longer safe for a little cat like me."

"They're not safe for anyone anymore," Haru said. "Those humans were not human."

Penelope shuddered delicately. "They were the ones attacked by the monster dogs."

She stared curiously into Haru's face. "But why is it they looked so different from you?" she asked. "They looked hideous and they smelled like death. You don't. It's very curious."

Haru heaved a sad breath. "Whatever was done to them was far worse than what was done to me."

"But what really happened to you, Haru?" she asked. "Your wounds heal quickly. You have unnatural strength and speed. The other dogs were just as strong, but they look like unnatural things."

"I'm not sure," Haru replied. "All I know is that when I first saw you after the bad place, I was almost like them. Like Bruno. But it was the memory of Luke that kept me from turning into a monster like they did. And that is why I must always protect my family. Because they also protect me."

Luke woke up and rubbed his eyes.

"Where are we going?" he asked.

"We're heading to New Jersey, to your uncle John and aunt Virginia's house," his dad replied. "It'll be another four hours at least."

"How long have we been driving?" Lydia asked with a yawn. "I'm sorry I didn't stay awake to help you. That allergy medicine made me so drowsy."

"That's okay, honey. It's been almost three hours," his dad said. "You both should keep sleeping. We're almost to the beltway that loops around Washington, DC, and will take us to Maryland. I don't want to stop for the night until we're far from Virginia."

Luke shuddered. "Good idea."

Traffic suddenly slowed to a complete halt.

"What's going on here?" Peter rolled down his window and stuck his head out. "I see flashing lights and lots of barricades. There's some kind of blockade up ahead."

"Dad, look!" Luke pointed to the left where a caravan of military vehicles was speeding down the highway. Trucks and Humvees and even tanks drove in formation down Interstate 66.

"They must be going to help the town," Luke said.

"I hope they're not too late," Peter sighed.

"Honey, Patricia texted us," Lydia said in alarm. "There was a mandatory evacuation order of Painted Lake and all the surrounding counties. She said there are military blockades along the entire Virginia border. They know about the dog attacks and they're not letting any dogs leave the state."

Luke grabbed Haru tight. "No," he sobbed.

His mom and dad turned to face Haru.

"Quick, get down, Haru," Lydia said. Haru obediently jumped to the floor.

"We're about ten cars away," Peter said grimly. "Luke, grab the blanket in the back and hide Haru underneath and tell him to be quiet."

Shaking, Luke unbuckled his seat belt and reached over to find the heavy gray moving blanket his father used for padding the trunk of the car when he went supply shopping.

"Haru, you have to hide and keep quiet," he said. "Hide. Quiet. Please."

Haru lay down on the floor under Luke's feet and Luke covered him completely with the blanket. Luke then sat back down and rested his feet lightly on the lump. Gathering Penelope into his arms, Luke hugged her tight, trying to keep his trembling in check.

His father put on the radio and boppy pop music filled the car, at odds with the tenseness of the passengers. They drove slowly as the cars ahead passed through the blockade one by one. The minutes felt like hours as Luke prayed that Haru would not give himself away. Two cars were now left in front of them. Suddenly, they heard the sound of barking as soldiers confiscated a small dog from the first car.

"Please, give me back my Teddy! There's nothing wrong with him!" A woman jumped out of the passenger side and tried to take back her dog, but the soldiers pushed her away.

"Sorry, we have orders to confiscate any dog," a soldier

replied. "Get back in your vehicle now."

The distraught woman was pulled back into the car by her husband. Now there was only one vehicle before them. Luke watched as the soldiers used flashlights to check inside the car before allowing the driver to leave.

And then it was their turn. Luke closed his eyes to pretend he was sleeping as his father drove up to the barricade and rolled down his window.

"Can we see your license, sir?" the soldier asked.

Peter handed his license to the soldier, who looked it over keenly before giving it back.

"And where are you going?"

"Going to my brother-in-law's place in Rahway, New Jersey," Peter said. "We took off as soon as we heard about the incident at the Sinclair factory."

The soldier pointed his flashlight into their car. Luke could see the brightness behind his eyelids, but he kept his eyes closed.

"Could you both please step out of the car," the soldier ordered.

Peter and Lydia slowly unbuckled their belts and exited their vehicle.

"Your son too," the soldier said.

"He's sleeping. It's been a frightening ordeal for him; please let him sleep," Peter said.

There was a long silence before the soldier asked, "What is he holding?"

"It's our cat, Penny," Peter said.

The soldier peered closely at Luke for a long moment before handing Peter a clipboard and asking him to write his name and his destination address. After several more minutes, Peter was finally able to return to the car and drive away.

It wasn't until they were safely on the beltway that they all breathed a sigh of relief.

"Let's keep Haru hidden until we're in Maryland," Peter said.

Luke lifted the blanket slightly and whispered, "Good boy."

As soon as they were on I-95 northbound in Maryland, Luke took off the heavy blanket and Haru jumped back onto the seat.

"Sorry, Haru," Luke said as he hugged Haru tight.

On the radio, a breaking news report interrupted the music.

"A mass evacuation is happening in the Common-wealth of Virginia due to a rapidly spreading disease causing sickness and death. It appears to be spread by rabid dogs. Virginia is in a military lockdown with no one allowed in."

"Mom, Dad, what's going to happen?" Luke asked.

"I don't know," Peter sighed. "But no matter what happens, we're going to get as far away as possible and stay safe. We'll make a new home for all of us."

Luke nodded and patted Haru's back. "Haru will keep us safe."

Penelope blinked and then climbed on top of Haru and fell asleep.

Home, Haru thought. *Home is where Luke is.*

FRIGHTFUL ACKNOWLEDGMENTS

HARU: ZOMBIE DOG HERO

Presented by HarperCollins' House of Horrible Children

Supreme Zombie Wrangler Writer—Ellen Oh

All the thanks in the world for the following brilliant,
talented, amazing, awesome people:

Queen of Editing Darkness—Alyson Day
Agent of Monstrosities—Marietta B. Zacker
Grim Editorial Assistants—Karina Williams, Eva
Lynch-Comer
Bloodsucking Copyeditors— Susan VanHecke, Susan
Bishansky, Kathryn Silsand, and Betsy Kennedy

Ghoulish Art Director—Joel Tippie
Knight of Nightmares Cover Artist—Teo Skaffa

Harper Team Coven— Vaishali Nayak, Jacqueline Burke, Delaney Heisterkamp, and Katie Boni
The Kraken Boss Lady—Suzanne Murphy

The Oh House of Terrors:
Grimly Graysin
Shrieking Skye
Savage Summer
Count Tokki-la
Frankenpup Kiko
Evil Emperor Darth Sonny